FLY FISHING THE RIVER STYX

Fly Fishing The River Styx

Stories With An Angle

by

RICHARD DOKEY

BOOKS

Adelaide Books
New York/Lisbon
2018

FLY FISHING THE RIVER STYX
stories with an angle
By Richard Dokey

Published by Adelaide Books, New York / Lisbon
adelaidebooks.org

Editor-in-Chief
Stevan V. Nikolic

For any information, please address Adelaide Books
at info@adelaidebooks.org
or write to:
Adelaide Books
244 Fifth Ave. Suite D27
New York, NY, 10001

ISBN-13: 978-1-949180-49-7
ISBN-10: 1-949180-49-2

Printed in the United States of America

In memory of Jack Dokey

Brother of all my rivers

Contents

Richard Dokey

Fly Fishing The River Styx

We sat at the campfire. Beyond the cone of flame, we heard the paw of water against stone and the vague stir of night awakening.

Charlie was at the drift boat tending to the gear. He had set up the tent and the mess table. He had staked the canvas bucket with water. He had dug the hole for the toilet and had placed a hinged bench above the hole. Charlie—we had already forgotten his last name—was our guide out of the life we had left behind.

We were fly fishermen, my brother Frank and I. As boys, learning from our father, we had fished the high Sierra. We had become men, had married, sired children, divorced and grown old, and on the way we had fished in Patagonia. We had fished in New Zealand, Alaska and Canada. We had fished the Rockies and the chalk streams of Britain. We had fished the rivers of Russia and Africa. And now we were far north, on a five-day float along a river accessible only by float plane, from one blue lake to the other, a sixty-mile drift through barren tundra, where no man lived and the trout were like footballs. We had heard rumors about the river. We had heard stories about the river. The river was bleak and unreal. It steamed in the morning light. At sundown it became blacker than night. It was the dream of every fly fisherman. The wives were history.

We had finished with the lawyers. We had set up the trusts. Give it all to the kids.

"I expect you boys are hungry," Charlie said, coming to stand by the fire. He was tall, of an age when age cannot accurately be determined. He had a full beard speckled with gray. The gray caught the firelight. It seemed to burn in the firelight. Yet Charlie was completely bald.

During the day, at the bow, as we floated and caught trout, I had looked into Charlie's eyes, which were jet black and set far into his head. His brows were black too, gnarled forward, like shrubs, and marked by the gray of his beard, so that his face seemed confused by time. He rowed effortlessly, sitting between us, now pushing with one oar, now pulling with the other, the boat pointed straight downriver, exactly in the center so that we could reach either bank with a long cast. He was the best oarsman I had ever seen.

Charlie lifted the lid from a Styrofoam box. He removed two skillets and a cutting board. He had saved two large trout from late in the day. He filleted the trout.

Charlie diced four large potatoes, leaving on the skins. He chopped an onion and a red bell pepper. Magically he made corn bread in a hot urn. He covered the fillets with flour, salt and pepper. He splashed a layer of olive oil into the skillet and slid the fillets into the oil. The fillets popped and hissed. They created a lovely smell. The potatoes were in the other skillet, popping and hissing.

Charlie put a cup of ground coffee into a blackened aluminum pot. He put the pot against the fire. He opened a can of condensed milk.

The darkness beyond the fire was black. Frank and I waited. We watched as Charlie moved things around with a wooden spoon, making it all come out right. Now he wore a frayed oven mitt. It was probably the original oven mitt. Charlie didn't say a word.

When he was done, Charlie portioned everything into three aluminum trays, the kind in use at cafeterias. He poured the coffee into three aluminum mugs. He set the can of condensed milk between us.

We sat on the campstools eating. I had camped out many times with my own kids and with Frank and his kids. Frank was a fair cook himself. We had produced many camp dinners. We had fried trout and potatoes. But this from Charlie was truly fine. Beneath absolute night, Frank and I and Charlie the guide, just the three of us for hundreds of miles of blunt wilderness, sat about a primitive fire, eating food that we had captured, on a journey that began in solitude and would end the same way.

When we were done, having eaten all that had been prepared and having consumed the entire pot of coffee, Charlie uncovered an earthen jug. He rinsed the cups and filled the cups from the jug.

"What is it?" I asked. I raised the cup to my nose. The liquid smelled sweet and strong.

"My special brew," Charlie said. "I make it for these trips."

"What is it?" Frank said.

"I won't tell you that. But you'll like it. Trust me. It's good after a meal, way out here."

"Is it whiskey or gin or like what?" I asked. "What do you mix with it, Charlie?" I took a sip. It was sweet and hot. It went down sweet and hot. It came to rest in my stomach. It reminded me of being naked.

"It's great," Frank said.

I finished the cup. It became easier with each swallow. I held the cup out. Charlie refilled it.

"You won't think of anything now," Charlie said. "You're just fishermen."

I looked at Frank. Frank smiled and held out his cup. I produced three cigars. We lit up and drank more of Charlie's brew. It was sweet and not hot at all. It lay in my stomach like a great warm melon burst open. It was a warm naked melon lying inside me.

Charlie smoked his cigar. He smiled.

"You boys will do," he said. "You're all right."

"You get some that aren't, I suppose?" I asked.

"Some," he said. "There are all kinds. Some are all right."

"Well, thanks, Charlie," Frank said. "You're all right too."

Maybe Frank was thinking of our guides on the Tongariro in New Zealand and the Bighorn in Montana. Assholes. Real assholes.

"We're all all right," I said. "The three of us together. That's what's all right."

"That's all there is," Charlie said.

We sat smoking and trying to see through the night.

"So how long have you been at it, Charlie?" I asked.

"Out here, guiding?"

"Yes," I said. "Rowing old farts across the middle of no-where."

I was getting sleepy. Charlie put a little more of his brew into my cup. Frank held out his cup. The fire got smaller.

"All my damned life," Charlie replied. "That's how it seems."

"That's a long time," said Frank.

"That's all the time," Charlie said.

"Are you married?" I asked.

"I was never married."

"Why weren't you married?" I asked. "You'd think out here you'd want to be married. To have that to go back to, I mean."

"I never could be married," Charlie said.

"Well, women, then," Frank said. "In general, I mean."

"Generally, what about them?"

"You must get lonely," said Frank.

"Lonely," Charlie said. "Sure, sometimes I'm lonely, but then a couple of geezers like you come along."

I laughed. "It's empty out here, Charlie."

Charlie looked at the firelight.

"Oh, I don't know," Charlie said. "Not when I'm with fishermen."

"But you must get lonely," Frank pushed. Frank had chased women since the divorce. He had chased them for thirty years. Frank loved the hunt, as he called it. He wore Bermuda shorts on all but the coldest days and laid out for a tan. He was tan now. My legs were white. Frank wore leather sandals. Even his toes were tan. He was tan everywhere but his butt. He wore Jockey shorts to bed. I wore pajamas. He was an old fart who needed a tan.

"I get lonely sometimes," Charlie said, "but not the way you think of lonely."

"Which way, Charlie?" I asked.

"The way you are at a movie theater when you come out after the show."

I looked at Frank.

"But not with fly fishermen who know what to do," Charlie said, "and you're two of the best I've seen. You've been at it a while."

"Since we were kids," I said.

"All over, I suppose," Charlie said.

"We've been around," I replied.

"It shows," Charlie said, lifting his cup. "But never in a place like this. Not this far out."

"Never this far out, Charlie," said Frank.

"That's good," Charlie said. "That's the way it should always be. There should always be something more. That's why I'm never bored and never lonely, not truly."

"What do you mean?"

"Everyone is different, wouldn't you say? But this is the same. You come to it the way you are. I watch the difference. All my clients are different, but out here it's the same thing. See what I mean? So I don't see the river anymore. All I see are the clients and how they fish. You boys are good fishermen."

We were almost asleep. I felt proud. I'd been fly fishing all my life, and it was still like the first day. If you do one thing, again and again—cast a fly, catch a trout—time loses its individuality. Time isn't time.

"I'll bet you have plenty of stories," Frank said.

"I do have stories," he said.

"Tell us one, Charlie."

"Why can't that wait?" he said, standing.

"Just one, Charlie," Frank said. "Come on."

"Tomorrow's another day, boys. There are days beyond that."

"I'm sleepy anyway," I said.

"Sure you are," Charlie said. "I'll see you boys in the morning."

Only one two-man tent had been set up.

"Where are you going to sleep?" I asked.

"On the ground," Charlie said. "I always sleep on the ground."

"But the dew. Won't you get wet?"

"I have a tarp for under my bag and a rig to cover my head. I can't sleep inside a tent. Never could. Good night, boys."

We walked to the tent and threw back the flap. I realized that Charlie had not used my name. It felt a bit odd to be talked to so long and not hear my name. He had not used Frank's name. We were anonymous. Generic.

Charlie provided a small kerosene lamp. It hung from a peg. Frank removed a plastic box from his kit. I removed my plastic box. The boxes had compartments. In the compartments were the pills. Frank had more pills than I had. Pink ones. Yellow ones. White ones, Lipitor. Blood pressure. Thyroid. Aspirin. We downed them with the sweet flame of Charlie's brew. We had entered the Age of Medicine. The Age of Continual Care.

Frank crawled into his bag. I put on my flannel pajamas and rolled my pants and shirt together for a pillow. I peeked through the flap. Charlie sat at the fire, hunched over, an aluminum cup in one hand, his cigar in the other. Smoke curled from his head, like the gray ghost of a soul. I dropped the flap, crawled into my bag and zippered it shut. I went into a sleep deeper than dirt.

In the morning we woke to the smell of bacon and hot coffee. I threw back the tent flap. Charlie was at the fire flipping pancakes.

We hurried into our clothes and out into the morning air.

"'Morning, boys," Charlie said. "Sleep well?"

"Like rocks," Frank said.

Charlie smiled and nodded. "How many pancakes?"

I rubbed my hands. "Keep 'em coming, Charlie. Keep 'em coming."

"Eggs?"

"You bet," Frank said.

Mist came off the river. We couldn't see the river. The mist was a three-foot high, burly layer spread over either bank. The river was a gray mist that did not move, but we heard the river talking against the stones.

The dawn was behind us. It blanched the mist with a yellow veneer and went on to cap the horizon in a yellow glow. Above, the sky was white yellow. When I turned around, organdy rouge hung suspended above the sun.

"Do you ever get used to it, Charlie?" I asked.

Charlie looked up from the frying pan. He looked at the mist and the whitening sky.

"No," he said. "That's a fact. But after awhile you don't see it."

"What do you mean?" Frank said.

Charlie smiled. "You don't see it. Hand me your tray."

We ate the pancakes. We ate the bacon and eggs. We drank a pot of coffee. The mist lifted. The river was there, unhurried. Near the far bank, a trout rose.

Our rods were all set up. We put on our waders, struck camp and loaded everything into the drift boat. This time Frank got into the bow. I got into the stern. Charlie pushed the boat out with an oar. The boat was broad in the current. Charlie brought it around.

We began casting. The lines—mine was gray, Frank's was green—made tight bows, like harp strings strung one above the other. The tight bows uncurled, held for a moment, then dropped, the leader uncurling, the fly at the point of the tippet touching down like a dry leaf. The fly drifted with the current. Charlie held the boat true. The fly and the boat were together, drifting at the same speed.

The trout struck. They came out of the water, silver and blue, spotted orange and yellow. They fled downriver. They ground up against the current behind the boat. They were big trout, heavy trout. Charlie took them in his net. He released them into the water. Always the boat stayed true, centered in the current, drifting in the center of the river.

Sometimes I didn't fish. I watched Frank fish. I felt the thump, thump of the boat against the hide of the current. I watched the day come up. I watched Charlie row, effortlessly, like someone swimming with oars. I had never seen anyone row like Charlie.

Occasionally we stopped to fish a particularly good spot. Charlie knew these spots, deeper holes, long eddies and slicks. My arm throbbed with hooking and playing enormous trout.

My hand ached against the cork grip. I was delicious and tired, the way I felt after making love. I lay back on the pillow of trout fishing and closed my eyes.

Around noon Charlie oared the boat to the far bank. We jumped out. Charlie pulled the bow of the boat up onto the bank. He removed the camp table, the Styrofoam chest and the stools.

"Corn beef sandwiches, boys. Pickles. Onions. Gouda. Oranges. Homemade macaroons for dessert."

"Jesus," I said. "Who made the macaroons, Charlie?"

"I made them," Charlie said.

"Jesus."

We sat eating and watching the water. Springs flowed from the tundra into the river. Trout rose. Charlie filled our cups with his elixir. We drank and ate. Everything was warm and good.

"Say, Charlie," Frank said. "Why don't you fish too? We have extra rods. Come on. Fish with us."

"That's a great idea, Charlie," I said. "You fish too."

"I don't fish, boys," Charlie said.

"What do you mean?" I said. "You can fish."

"I know how to fish, but I don't. It's not my job to fish. My job is to serve my clients. I row the boat and put you over big trout. That's what I'm paid to do. I'm not paid to catch fish."

"Well, these clients say it's okay to fish, Charlie. We want you to fish," Frank said. "Give us a rest. Have a turn."

"I won't fish, boys," Charlie said. "But, say, I'll take another cigar."

After a bit we climbed into the boat, Frank in the stern, though I had had the bow all the day before.

"I don't work so hard back here," Frank said.

So now both Charlie and I were faced away from Frank, and when I looked back sometimes, Frank was not fishing. He leaned against the stern brace, smiling.

The day went on. I fished to the point of fatigue. Some times Frank fished. He whooped and fought the trout. He yelled, turning the rod this way and that against the pull of the trout. But it seemed harder to get them in. Charlie had the net in the water, but Frank was content to let the trout swim about the river.

"Lift the rod," Charlie said. "Higher."

Frank muscled the trout. He was sweating. I watched Charlie's face after he released Frank's fish. He watched my face. So I was old. So Frank was old. I wondered if Charlie knew just how old we were.

That night, ten miles further downriver, we sat at the fire. We drank Charlie's brew. Charlie had saved two more trout. This time he smothered the fillets in garlic and onion. He made a salad from a bag of vegetables. He made biscuits in the urn. He took out a jar of honey.

"Hold out your trays, boys."

Charlie filled my tray. Frank put a hand over his, measuring small portions.

"Not too hungry right now," Frank said. "Stomach's a little upset. I'll just have this."

So we ate. Charlie didn't tell stories. We talked about fishing and a world where there were no trout. We talked about the country. I brought out the cigars, but Frank said, "I'll pass. Go ahead. I'm a bit tired. I think I'll sack out early."

Frank went to the tent. He threw back the flap and crawled in. He closed the flap.

Charlie and I sat smoking. We didn't talk much. I was tired too. I was more tired than I thought I was. This was hard work for old farts that need Viagra. Charlie wasn't tired. He sat at the fire, smoking and drinking. Maybe one day he would be tired too. Maybe one day he would stop rowing.

"Well, guess I'd better turn in too," I said. I wanted to pat Charlie on the back, but I didn't touch him. "Thanks, Charlie," I said. "It was a great day. It was the best day of fishing I ever had."

He looked at me. "That's good," he said. "And you're not done yet."

I nodded and went to the tent. I drew back the flap. Frank was in his bag, curled against the far wall. I took my pills and got into my bag. I looked out at Charlie. He sat at the fire smoking his cigar. A gray ghost rose from his head. He still had not called either of us by name.

The next morning I awoke to the smell of coffee and bacon. I lay in the bag. I kept my eyes closed, thinking about the coffee and the bacon, the pancakes and the eggs. I was content to keep my eyes closed and to think.

Then Charlie called, "The trout are rising, boys! No rest for the wicked!"

I looked at Frank. He was curled against the tent. I unzipped my bag. I reached over and pushed Frank.

Frank moaned.

I scrambled from my bag. I bent over Frank. I moved him a little. His head turned.

Frank's eyes were back, rolling and looking. The corners of his mouth were wet.

"Jesus," he said. "I'm sick. My shoulder. My arm."

I threw back the flap of the tent. "Charlie!" I yelled. "Charlie!"

Charlie ran over. He got to his knees. He looked at Frank. He looked at me.

"Something happened," I said. "Something's wrong."

Charlie looked closely into Frank's face.

"He wasn't so good before," Charlie said. "He looked ill."

"What is it?" I said. "What happened?"

"I don't know," Charlie said. "Something. Maybe stroke. Maybe heart."

"Charlie," I said, "what do we do?"

Charlie said, "I don't know what to do. If it's inside, there's nothing to do. Make him comfortable."

"What is it?" Frank muttered. "What happened?" His eyes were bulged forward in a look of terror.

"Charlie," I said, "we must get back. We have to get out of here."

"Put your gear on," Charlie said. "I'll load the boat while you eat."

"Eat? Frank may be dying. We've got to get help."

"Get dressed," Charlie said. "We'll put him in the stern of the boat and keep him still. That's what we can do. You eat. What good is not eating? I'm going to eat."

I dressed. We struck camp. We put Frank into the back of the boat. We put him on a tarp. We made a pillow of things. He was in his sleeping bag, shivering, eyes wide and looking.

"Charlie!" I cried.

He came to me. He stood in front of me, "Eat!" he declared.

"We've got to get back!" I yelled.

"And if I row all day and all night and we don't sleep or eat and we get back to the take-out early, what then?"

"We leave. We get Frank back to a doctor. He's ill."

"The plane won't be back for three days," Charlie said.

"Call them," I said. "Call them on a radio or a phone or something. Tell them to come and get us."

"Nothing works out here," Charlie said. "It's too far out. We wait. That's how it is. You might just as well fish."

"What?"

"Fish. That's why you're here, isn't it?"

"How in hell can I fish when my brother might be dying? In God's name, Charlie!"

"What else can you do?" said Charlie.

I stared into his eyes. They were big, black eyes set into his head. His scruffy black brows almost touched his eyes.

"Charlie," I said.

He gripped my arm. He held me. I couldn't move.

"Would you rather fish while you wait," Charlie said, "or would you rather just wait?"

I ate breakfast. I got into the bow of the boat. Charlie shoved off.

We drifted. The river steamed. In the stern Frank moaned in his sleeping bag, his eyes wide, looking straight up at the empty sky.

I lifted my rod. Trout were rising on either side. I snapped the line out to the far shore.

I fished all morning. At midday Charlie handed me a sandwich and a cup of brew. I fished into the afternoon.

I stood in the bow of the boat. My brother was on a tarp in the stern. The fly line was a hot wire. I released it, out over the water. I fished all day and into the evening. I was exhausted with fishing. I had never caught so many trout.

"I want to tell you," Charlie said, as the sun met the horizon, "you're the best damned fly fisherman I've ever seen, and I've seen them all."

And still Charlie rowed.

Something Big

They took the leg off below the knee. He lay in the hospital bed looking at the ceiling. He had read how people sometimes still felt a leg, a kind of ghost leg, but a leg nevertheless. Or an arm, an arm you could not see, but still feel. With something small, a toe, maybe, a finger, it was not that way. It had to be big. It was impossible to accept that so much of you was in a bucket or wrapped in a bag somewhere. You had this aura leg or phantom leg. You wiggled invisible toes.

A curtain was fastened to an aluminum rod between the two beds in the room. A groan came from the other bed. The curtain drew back. Dr. Andrade looked down at him.

"Well, Greg," Andrade said, "and how are we feeling this morning?"

He did not know how the doctor felt, but he knew how he felt.

"Let's have a look, then," the doctor said.

Greg raised his head. His left foot pushed up the blankets. Nothing was below the knee of the right leg. The blankets were flat against the bed.

"Pain, Greg?" the doctor asked, moving the blanket.

"Not much," he said. "Numbness mostly."

"You let the nurse know if you have pain. We have many things for pain. What did you enjoy doing before?"

"I was a fly fisherman," he said, looking at the curtain.

"You will fly fish again. With the healing and time and the prosthetic device, you will fish whenever you like. You will be a champion of fly fishing. Do you believe that?"

He tried to smile. A groan came from the other bed.

"Unfortunate," the doctor said. "He was drunk on the freeway. He struck a bridge abutment at seventy miles an hour. Crushed below the pelvis." He looked carefully at Greg. "And now you must rest."

His two sons came. They sat on the bed, one on each side. They agreed that removing the leg was the correct thing. The wound in the heel, after so much time, simply would not close, and the infection had spread up the leg. Nothing was anyone's fault, of course, or maybe it was merely the fault of being born with the blood disease. He was a trial lawyer who could no longer stand in court. He had gone on permanent disability. Now he was a lawyer with one leg. His sons had not been interested in fly fishing. Sitting on the bed talking, they wanted to become fly fishermen and would he please teach them when he got well.

Beverly, their mother, had not succeeded in contaminating them, spiritually, anyway. She did not come to the hospital. The divorce three years before had been vituperative. He supposed she was doing now what she had always wanted to do, and he was glad not to hear about it. He did not want her on the bed, smelling like the perfume counter at Macy's and working hard to be soft. They sold everything. She moved into the town house. He bought the truck and the fifth wheel.

It was fall. The trailer was parked in the lot behind the casino. The casino permitted him to keep it there in the winter. He liked to play poker. It was good to stay competitive. He baked brownies and cream pies for the dealers and pit bosses.

When he wasn't gambling, he tied flies. He had the nose of the trailer converted for fly typing. There was a bench and drawers for materials, hooks, feathers and hair. He tied dozens of flies at a sitting. He was pretty good at fly tying. Some of the fishermen he met paid him to tie flies for them. It was good to be useful and in demand. He enjoyed inventing new patterns and trying them out wherever he fished. Everybody liked his flies. He was a trout bum. He lived in a trout bum's trailer. It was what he had always wanted to do.

He wanted to see the stump, but could not bring himself to move the blankets.

Later, of course, he did see the stump. He was propped up in bed. The doctor removed the bandages, bent close and touched the flesh with the tip of his finger.

The doctor said, "Greg?"

He felt a pain so immediate that it was as though the doctor had touched his brain. The stump was kneaded, like potter's clay, swollen and red.

"I'm sorry," the doctor said. "I know it is quite tender. Would you like something?"

"Yes," he said.

"It looks fine, though," the doctor said. "It is better than fine, I would say. It is quite fine indeed. When the swelling comes down and the pain is gone, we will begin the therapy. I am very much encouraged, Greg. You will be the champion of all fly fishing. I guarantee it."

He smiled. The doctor smiled too. The doctor made a fresh dressing and gave him a shot. He lay back. Nothing was like pain when pain went away.

The next day men in white coats came to remove the freeway accident. A sheet covered the gurney. The man was drunk. He had killed himself. Others were spared. I am lucky, he thought. It was not my casting arm or my eyes. In a float tube I will be the champion of fly fishing.

After a time Marlene came to the hospital.

"I would have come sooner," she said. "But I'm having so much trouble now with Ray."

"How is it, then?" he asked.

"The same," she said. "More so."

"I'm sorry to hear that," he said.

Marlene, Ray, Beverly and he had met at the University. They had been great pals. They did everything together. They even got married together. When they paired off finally, he wondered, at the time, who had gotten the better deal.

Marlene sat on the edge of the bed.

"It's impossible to bring him, then, I suppose," he said.

"Greg, he wouldn't know who you were. He doesn't know who I am. He comes into a room. 'Where's my wife?' he yells. 'I want my wife.' I want to cry. I've lived in that house with him for thirty years. He makes messes now. He takes things out of cupboards and drawers and drops them on the floor so he can find his way back. And he yells, Greg. 'Where is she? Where is my wife?' Until even I don't know where she is. Sometimes, when he's asleep, I go into the bedroom. I look at him. His face is so soft, the way it was. Sometimes I think he'll wake up and say, 'Hey, Honey, what's for dinner?' When he wakes up, I'm small and useless. I'm going crazy living with a madman."

"Jesus," he said. He looked at the blanket and felt grateful.

"Enough about that," she said, wiping her face. "Our daughter Kathy's with him so I can come see you. How are you doing, Greg? Are you all right?"

"It beats the alternative, doesn't it?" he said.

"What's the doctor say?"

"He says what doctors say. Rehab. Therapy. A new leg. A nice metal leg, chrome plaited, with a life-time warranty. If it gets rusty or fails to perform, I get a new leg, no charge." He smiled. "I'm having two made, one for fly fishing and the other for dancing."

"Oh, Greg."

"I'm going to be the champion of fly fishing. The doctor guarantees it."

"You'll fish again?"

"Have to," he said. "When I get the hang of it, that is. No pun intended."

"You're silly, "she said. "That's such good news. They can replace everything these days. Heart. Liver. Lungs. And it's only part of a leg."

"Enough of a leg," he said, "so I can still get to the can."

"Oh, Greg, that's the way," she said, "That's how to be."

She burst into tears.

"Marlene," he said.

"Greg, why must we bear so much? We have done nothing, nothing at all. I feel so guilty and so helpless."

"It's nobody's fault. Didn't you just say that?"

"I know," she said. "But what difference does it make? I've been with Ray all these years. And now he's there, but he's not there anymore."

"There are places," he said.

"Certainly, there are places, but do you want me to feel even more guilty? It's Ray, even if it's not Ray."

She put her face against the bed. He stroked her hair. He recalled the time, a year before, when he had stayed three days with Ray while Marlene attended her daughter's graduation back East.

Ray strode into the living room, where he sat reading a magazine.

"You want a Snickers?" Ray said, holding out a box.

"No, Ray. No, thanks," he said.

"Who are you?" Ray said. "What are you doing here? Why don't you want a Snickers?"

"Marlene will be back soon, Ray," he said.

"You don't like Snickers," Ray said.

"I like Snickers," he said. "I just don't feel like a Snickers right now, Ray."

"Where's the woman who lives here? Where did she go?"

"She'll be back in a while, Ray."

"Who are you? I demand to know. Why don't you want a Snickers?"

He stared at his old friend.

"A Milky Way," Ray said. "I have Tootsie Rolls and Milky Ways. You want a Tootsie Roll or a Milky Way?"

"All right, Ray," he said. "I'll have a Milky Way."

Ray took a Milky Way from the box. They sat in the room eating candy. Then Ray stood up. A stain was between his legs.

"I have to go," Ray said.

He helped Ray to the bathroom.

Marlene raised her head. "Oh, look at me," she said. "I'm so sorry, Greg.

"Listen," he said, "why don't I get the feel of my new leg. I have all winter and spring. Let's make a plan. Let's go fly fishing together. I'll teach you how to catch trout. The great outdoors and all. Would you like that?"

"Fly fish?" she said. "Me?"

"Sure. Why not? Since I can't walk a stream anymore, we'll float in tubes. I have just the place. We sit in a harness and just drift along. There's nothing more relaxing than fishing from a tube. Get someone to stay with Ray, someone professional. There are people who do that sort of thing. Silver Creek in Idaho on Memorial Day. We'll fish the brown drake hatch. The big trout come up for the drakes. I'll get you a room above the old Picabo store. It's close to the creek. I'll set you up. The creek is like a bathtub. We'll float along. I'll show you how to cast. You'll love it. I guarantee you'll love it. What do you say? It's impossible to fish and think of something else."

"I don't know," she said. "Do you think I could?"

"I know you could. I know you'll love it. Remember the old days? How the four of us used to camp out and hike the trails around Yosemite? You love the outdoors. It's just what the doctor ordered. I'll park my trailer at Point of Rocks. I keep it there. Point of Rocks is right on the creek. We'll fish. I'll fix Cornish game hens for dinner. We'll drink wine. We'll listen to trout splashing in the water. I have a stereo. We'll listen to Delius. We'll listen to Chopin. The next day, we'll do it all over again."

Her face was bright.

"I'll have the winter and spring to get used to the leg. I know I can do it. It will be fine. I'm inspired."

"You really think it would be all right, Greg? That I should even consider it, I mean?"

"Consider it? Do it, Marlene. You'll love it. Guaranteed."

The leg was a metal rod the circumference of a wading staff. A cup mechanism, open in front and behind, fit over the stump, help by straps. There was a foot, a flesh-colored thing that reminded him of a shoe tree or the foot of a mannequin. The wading staff was articulated where the ankle used to be. In the place of toes there was a painted facsimile of toes.

He wore the leg. A male nurse held him under one arm. He walked on the foot. Then he walked alone. He walked outside on the lawn and up and down stairs. He balanced on the foot. It was strange seeing the metal rod glint in the sunlight. It was odd watching the articulation work. The metal rod was a bone without flesh. The foot had no feel. He wore a special shoe over the foot and long pants, but the knee could not do what a knee did. The leg was something from a hardware store. The foot sounded hollow when it struck the floor.

But it was not a phantom leg. He went to the bathroom with the leg and into the shower with the leg. It wasn't his casting arm. It wasn't his eyes. It was part of a leg. Once he faced it, it wasn't a big thing at all.

In the spring he was able to walk into the casino. The pit bosses, the dealers and the regulars knew what he had gone through. They tried not to look, but they looked. He raised the pant leg to show them the rod. It shone in the yellow light. He was not embarrassed, he told them.

"I'm lucky," he said. "Look. No hair."

Everyone laughed. They played poker.

By the end of May he had the trailer at Silver Creek. The room was ready above the Picabo store. When Marlene's plane landed at Sun Valley Airport, he was there to meet her.

"How do you drive, then?" she asked, after he had put her things in the back of the truck.

"I don't have feeling in the artificial foot, of course. I had the gas petal shifted to the left side. I use my left foot to go. It's called prosthetic driving. How's Ray?"

"We're not to talk about Ray, Greg."

"All right," he said. "I'll get you to your place. You can freshen up. We'll have dinner at Da Vinci's in Hailey. In the morning I'll pick you up. We'll have breakfast at the trailer."

"That sounds fine," she said. "And I don't mean it about Ray. I just want to smell this air. Isn't it marvelous?"

The following morning they drove to the Double R Ranch, which was his favorite place on the creek. He struggled with the gear.

"Let me help with something, Greg," she said. "There must be something I can do." She watched the water.

"I'll manage," he said.

He helped her with the waders he had bought for her in Ketchum. He struggled into his own waders. He hobbled to the bank and tried to see exactly how to proceed. He decided to put the tube into the water, step into the harness with his good leg, then get the other leg in as best he could. It took some doing. He was panting. Marlene was in the water waiting.

He decided not to fish. He showed her about the casting and about presentation and a drag-free drift. Trout were rising in the middle of the creek. The creek was not deep. The tubes were for covering the water, positioning above a rising fish, planting the feet against the silty bottom and then feeding the fly down to the trout. It felt good to explain it all and to show her everything and to float free in the soft current. The water was cool in the warm Idaho sun. He taught her to cast and how to set the hook when the trout struck.

He felt very professional. He watched her face. He watched the softness come. She drifted beside him in the sunlight. After a time, it did not matter if she fished or not. The water was cool. The air was clean.

They were on the creek three hours. They reached the take-out. He explained about releasing the harness, about getting the tube up over her hips and climbing up out of the water. She managed with little difficulty. He passed her the fly rods.

He struggled with the tube. It had been relatively easy to get into the water, but now he was having difficulty. He tried to lever himself with the good leg, then draw the other leg out of the harness. He tried planting the other leg in the silty bottom, but he had no feeling. The leg slipped back. He looked at her, his eyes bright and desperate, his face aflame. He planted both feet and lifted the tube, trying to maneuver it high enough so that he could fall forward across it. The bank was high. The leg slipped.

"Greg," she said, "what can I do?"

Panting, cursing, he threw himself over the tube, clawing at the grassy bank, shoving with the good leg. She tried to pull him under the arms. He was heavy. She only succeeded in hurting him. He dug his fingers into the grassy bank. He pulled and shoved, then lay across the tube, out of the water. He rolled onto his back, exhausted, blinking into the sun.

She helped him out of the waders. He tried to stand.

"Would you go back for the truck, Marlene?" he said. "I don't think I can make it."

"Yes, of course," she said.

He handed her the keys. The river had made many "s" curves. In a straight line, if she cut across the field, it was only a quarter mile to the truck.

"It's so damned embarrassing, Marlene," he said. "Everything was going so well. I didn't think it would be so tough getting out."

"You rest," she said. "I'll manage the truck."

Back at the trailer, they had a drink. He felt better. He prepared the dinner. They sat at the tiny table inside eating the game hens and drinking wine. Then they sat on the folding chairs outside and watched the trout rising in the creek.

"Greg," she said after a time, "will you please not drive me back to the store tonight."

He pushed out of the chair and climbed into the trailer. She followed. He shut the door.

He went to the bed and sat down. He removed the pants. He removed the artificial leg. The stump was bruised, naked and red.

"No pity," he said.

"No pity," she replied.

Patagonia

There were six of us, Mitch Adler, who was leading the group, a wealthy, fat realtor named Cecil Billingsly, Glenn Roule, retired from the Department of Fish and Game, Alan Chadwick, a banker, my brother Frank and I.

The first day out I thought the country so much like the hills of Montana along the Yellowstone below Livingston or those beneath the Sierra Nevada above the San Joaquin Valley that I said to Frank, "What does this remind you of?"

"See for yourself," he said.

"So we came thousands of miles and spent thousands of dollars to catch fish no bigger than what we'll get on the Bighorn in August? Is that it?"

He shrugged. "What else are you going to do with your money?"

Our guide, a short, quick, black-eyed young man named Ernesto, whose waders fit a like gunny sack tied with a string, led us to the Rio Simpson, where we fished stimulators, royal Wulffs and, at dusk, caddis came off in the huddled shadows under the trees. Frank hooked a 24-inch brown he couldn't see, striking when Ernesto called, "Now," fighting for twenty minutes until, darkened and the camera back in the room, we held a beautifully spotted creature, with nothing but memory to tell it had happened, and that already going with the light. Later, near eleven, we sat around an elegantly appointed table at the lodge. Our host, John Cole, an expatriate from Vermont, raised a crystal goblet of red wine.

"Your arrival at the heart of Patagonia," he declared. "New adventures. New friends."

We drank. I watched Mitch leer at Cole's wife Adriana.

Perched at the other end of the table, long, soft-black hair curled about cream-colored shoulders, perfect, dark features and eyes that came to you like those from a painting by Velasquez, she seemed both near and distant, for she was pure Chilean and spoke no English.

We had beef that night. Comparisons were made. Everyone agreed it was as good or better than any we had eaten in the States. Cole's chef, a dough-faced woman who cooked at a local restaurant in the off-season, brought in the dessert, round, puffy cakes sprinkled with lemon rind and powdered sugar. Cec, seated to Adriana's left, gobbled three, wrapped two more in a paper napkin and put them into a breast pocket. Adriana smiled.

Then we were in the living area, which opened from the dining room, only the men, smoking, sipping brandy and lying about trout. A girl in a black uniform served coffee. I thought that Cole must be rich, family money, perhaps, but labor was cheap, I discovered. There were boys to take care of the grounds and dry our boots, someone to clean the house. It was all very efficient and caring and no feeling of servants, like a family. Our laundry was done each morning, the underwear ironed and folded. I named Cole El Patron.

The only guy I knew in the group, aside from my brother, of course, was Mitch, a retired rancher and fishing nut who worked part time at the fly shop that had put the trip together. Mitch sold me tying materials, gave me a discount on Tiemco hooks and was okay generally, but unashamedly raw, an old man with an old wife. His face wore lust the way a fat woman wears a cotton t-shirt.

Cec, glad at last to sit in a stuffed chair, his hands folded about a glass, his hair still damp from the shower he had luxuriated in after having quit early from the stream, marveled at the dinner he had been served, the tiny stuffed mushrooms, the scalloped potatoes and especially the pastry, which he compared to the best he had found anywhere in Sacramento, particularly Max's Opera Cafe, the hangout of his girlfriend, who, he laughed, probably wouldn't be around when he returned.

Glenn got into Cole at the table that first evening. It seemed that Glenn had a guiding service too, hauling people by mule and horse to fish for golden trout in the Sierra above Tuolumne Meadows. Glenn was past seventy and remarkably fit. Cole was thirty-five at most, so the old man couldn't abide somebody half his age offering him advice. But I'll give Glenn one thing. He must have been happily married or at least content, because I never saw him look hard at Adriana, not even when we all stood up from dinner and she pushed her chair back, leaning forward in a way that I thought would make poor Mitch lose a filling.

The one who really interested me, though, was the banker, Alan Chadwick, who wore matching thermal long johns under his walking shorts, and, that afternoon, when I asked him why, said that's how the guides in New Zealand did it. When I told him I'd fished the Tongariro for two weeks the year before, with all the Kiwis in the area up for the spawning run of rainbows out of Lake Taupo, and I'd never seen anyone dressed like that, he frowned and walked away to light one of the Cohibas he had uncovered in a cigar shop in Santiago. The rest of us had been married at least once, I found out later. But Alan had never indulged.

Which, of course, wouldn't directly explain what happened. But the way things are these days, we're supposed to believe that everything is particular, that there are no clues to a general theory of human desire, that nothing, therefore, is either good or bad and that the entomology of a streambed tells us more about how to hook trout than history does about how to understand men. It became evident to me quite soon that Alan Chadwick was one of the most affected persons I'd ever met.

The affectation continued the following morning. Mitch had been leant a number of new Sage rods with a less progressive action, for throwing big flies into a stiff wind. Since wind is always a problem in this part of the world, we were anxious to try them, but Alan, smiling graciously, said, no, that was all right, he'd stick with his bamboo, which he removed from a monogrammed leather case and which, when I flexed it, bent, like overcooked spaghetti.

"A Payne," I said, handing it to him.

"From an estate," he declared, smiling dumpily, the gap between his front teeth filled by a pink tongue.

"An estate," I said.

"Foreclosure. Had it restored."

"It's a classic," I agreed.

"Yes," he said, looking at Adriana, who had come out on the front step to watch us get ready.

We were pulling on waders, tying boots, checking fly boxes. Alan stood, legs apart, arms crossed, gazing at John's wife. We all wanted to look at her. Of course, we all did look, but surreptitiously, with respect, that frame men have devised to make a museum of desire. Except Mitch, whose red face was overt and crude and, therefore, irrelevant.

I watched Alan. He looked as though he had found a treasure, rarer than the cane rod he held so gingerly between the tips of his stubby fingers. As John parceled us out, two to fish a boca, two for the Rio Simpson again and Frank and I to a tiny stream near the Argentinean border, I studied the banker.

Pretending to check his gear, hat pulled low, he never took his eyes off Adriana. She was beautiful, it was true, but no more so than any number of women I had known, including the one waiting for me at home. Something was going on with the banker, and I grew apprehensive.

Frank and I went with Ernesto to fish Coyhaique Alto, a stream no wider than a bathtub, where big browns hid beneath undercut banks. I had never experienced anything quite like it. The trout threw themselves into the air, flopped upon the bank or burrowed into the black mud behind thick grass. Ernesto got down on his knees to horse them out. When he held them up, gills flaring, gold and orange spots dripping light, in a place with no trees but only this wandering ditch through open fields, I thought the trout were being shamed unnecessarily, and I was glad when we quit for lunch.

Ernesto set up a grille against some shrubs out of the sun. John's cook had prepared the food. We had a fine salad, home-made bread, barbequed lamb and a truly delicious red wine. I lay back and closed my eyes.

Long ago I gave up measuring success by how many fish I caught, how big they were or whether I beat everyone else in the camp. Even now I am trying to convince myself of an odd, new idea. As much as I love the struggle, the leaping flight of a wild trout with a fly in its mouth, a fly which I myself, with all the skill and cunning I possess, have fashioned, the pleasure of landing it, of holding it, if only for a moment in my trembling hands, might be forgone, that points might be snipped from hooks, that all that is necessary for knowledge to prevail over a wild will to live, is the strike itself. Nothing would be harmed, and that which is beautiful, unmarred by terror and death. I have thought that this may be what we are for, the promise of our crawl out of the element in which these primitive creatures still exist. But it may only be an ideal that no fisherman can reach, or, more correctly, merely the quirk of an ageing, jaded mind.

The sun moved from the eastern sky above Argentina. I fell asleep. When I awoke, Ernesto and Frank were in the tiny stream, and I was content, for a time, to rest in the warm shade and watch them hunt for trout.

Again, we were the last ones back, and it was ten-thirty before we sat down to dinner. The cook had prepared a dish of baked salmon and creamed pasta. There were tiny, brown-crusted biscuits with homemade jam. Our glasses were filled with a dry white wine. We ate greedily, devouring gourmet food like pigs, only to fall, sodden, into bed, so that we might rise at seven to have breakfast and do it all over again.

We talked about the day. Tastefully, John explored our successes and failures, so that he could determine where to send us the next morning. Glenn made critical remarks. Adriana, at the far end of the table, was beautiful, smiling and silent. Alan sat to her left, and it was a time before any of us noticed that he was picking at his dinner.

John asked, "Is everything all right?"

Alan was embarrassed but stoic, his face uncritical, yet certain, as though he had merely read through another proposal to borrow money and had reached the inevitable conclusion.

"I can't eat this late," he said, "and go to bed. I can't sleep."

I saw Adriana's eyes open a bit when John, face gone blank, set his wine glass down.

"Well, that's certainly no problem, then," he said. "We'll see that you eat before seven. We'll take care of it."

"You'll miss the evening rise," I smirked.

Adriana said something in Spanish that was too quick for me to make out, but at the sound of her voice, Alan became extremely nervous, excused himself from the table and went up to his room. After dinner the rest of us stepped down into living area for cigars and brandy.

It was midnight before Frank and I climbed the stairs.

Our room was located at the rear of the house, over the kitchen. Before that was a smaller room with a single bunk, where Glenn slept. Alan's room, with a double bed, was just at the head of the stairs, separated from Glenn by a small bath. Glenn had gone up earlier and was already undressed when Frank went in. The door to Alan's room was ajar. A light was on. I pushed the door open.

He sat on the edge of the bed, all his clothes on and his head in his hands. He hadn't noticed me. I started to back out but stopped, for I heard a sound, an odd, hunted little sound, like something trapped way back under the bed. In spite of myself, I was sorry.

"Say," I tried, "that's too bad."

He looked up. I don't think he saw me.

"Your stomach. About sleep, I mean. The dinner was great." His eyes returned. They occupied his face. He wet his lips.

"What did she say?" he asked.

"What?" I said.

"You understand Spanish. I've heard you speak to the guides and the servants. I simply cannot eat so late and sleep, that's all. What did she say?"

I had studied the language in school, enjoyed using what I could remember and had even made my way through Madrid and Barcelona on a trip to Spain a few summers before.

"Too fast," I said. "Couldn't make it out."

Air seemed to go out of him.

"It's a shame she can't speak English," I said.

"Oh, no, no," he replied, agitated. "That's fine. That's perfectly fine. Why should she speak English? It's we who should speak her language."

I stood for a moment.

"She is beautiful, isn't she?" I said.

I stared at him. His face was broad and shining.

"Say," I said carefully, "are you all right?"

"All right?" he said.

"Yes. You know."

"Go to bed," he answered, and lay down against the wall.

I thought about it a long time, listening to Frank snore. I thought Cole should know. But know what? That a pompous ass from California, made lonely by self-absorption, coveted Adriana? The fact that I was uncomfortable around Alan spoke as much about me as it did about him. He was no more a threat than, well, Mitch, whose mind turned women over like nude photographs. I put the plugs into my ears and fell asleep.

The next day Frank and I went with John to fish a boca, the mouth of a stream where it drops out of a lake. We sat in the front of a flat-bottomed skiff. John stood in back, a steel rod fixed to the throttle of the engine. The skiff slapped and popped against the surface, which was an intense blue. Mist gathered in the gullies of the hills. White fingers of water came down everywhere between amber-green trees and shrubs. It was a beautiful place, made more so by the experience of a privacy and quiet still available in a crowded world.

We fished all day, missing many more than we caught, but it didn't matter. After awhile there is no difference between trout and the places where they live.

When we returned, everyone was in the living room waiting. Everyone but Alan.

Glen had fallen into the Rio Simpson. His waders were inside out, drying by the fire. He was sitting in a cushioned chair, his head back and his eyes closed. Mitch stood at the hearth, his face empty, staring at the floor. Cec, who held a very tall drink in one puffy hand, got up from the sofa and went to the window.

"Well, hey, guys," Frank said, "we nailed 'em." He stood in the middle of the room, his face blunt and proud.

"What happened?" I said.

Nobody moved. Oblivious, Frank walked over to the liquor table.

"Mitch?" I said.

He waved a hand, gave me an embarrassed glance and turned to the fire.

The food arrived. We went to the table and sat down. After a time John came in. He hadn't bothered to clean up. Adriana didn't appear.

We ate quickly. No one made a sound, not even the girl who always filled our glasses, humming softly behind parted lips. When the cook brought in the dessert, a large, glistening strawberry and rhubarb pie, her face was as white as cloth.

Finally John rose and said in a voice like stone,

"Gentlemen, tomorrow morning I will decide who is to go where. Please, now, enjoy the fire."

He left.

I looked from one face to the other. Frank said, "What the hell?" Mitch and Cec, who slept below, turned away. Glenn went to the stairs.

"I'm going to have a brandy," Frank declared.

Slowly I followed Glenn up past Alan's door, which was shut tight.

"C'mon, now, Glenn," I said.

Glenn went to the bed and sat down. He looked as old as he was.

"What happened?" I asked.

"Nobody knows exactly."

"What did he do?"

"Something," he said, "very, very foolish."

I sat beside him and waited.

"From what we could figure out, because nobody speaks English around here except Ernesto, and you know how that is."

"Okay," I said.

"Alan wanted to come back early. We were together. He said he wasn't feeling well. He wanted to lie down. Ernesto said he would bring him here, leave me to keep fishing, then come right back. We'd have the rest of the day. He did that."

Glenn leaned back against the wall.

"Nobody saw anything," he said. "But somebody talked to Ernesto when we got back."

"What?"

Glenn took a breath. "He went into her room. He said he just wanted to see her. She was changing clothes. She was there with nothing on. He passed out."

"Jesus," I said.

"She went hysterical," Glenn said. "She screamed enough to wake the dead. The women ran in. They dragged him out by the heels and dumped him onto the front lawn. He woke and ran up to his room. Mitch talked to him there. That's it."

I thought about it. It was horrible enough, all right, but not irremediable. Alan was a fool, but not evil. "What about John? Does John understand?"

Glenn shrugged. "What's to understand?"

"What will he do?"

"What can he do? Alan was stupid. We have four more days to fish."

When I went in to tell Frank, he was asleep.

The next day Cec wasn't interested in fishing. He asked John if he might hire someone to drive him the twenty miles to the coast, where the Rio Simpson empties into the sea. Moving that weight in neoprene waders tired his legs, he complained, and he had brought plenty of money and wanted to spend some. That left Frank and me for the Nireguao, a meadowland stream noted for its grasshoppers, and Mitch and Glenn, with John, for the Boca Azul. John did not speak to Alan, who, in his odd costume, stood apart, head bowed, like an anchorite that had betrayed an oath. Ernesto, whom I had seen earlier talking with Adriana, both her hands around one of his brown arms, walked straight to Alan and took the leather rod case. "We are for the Rio Desague," I heard him say, a river none of us had yet seen.

Frank and I had good luck again, using only flies that I had tied, the Nireguao like the Trinity River in Northern California, but without trees. We fished straight into the sun. When the trout exploded out of the water, I thought a piece of the sky had torn apart.

When we returned that night, all the lights in the house were on, and everyone was waiting outside.

Alan was dead.

He had slipped, fallen against a rock, hit his head, rolled into the river and drowned. Ernesto had had a difficult time getting him back. The body was in town.

There were three days left, and I told John that I wanted Ernesto to guide Frank and me and that it didn't matter where we fished.

The evenings were as they had been. Adriana, more beautiful than ever, sat quietly across from her husband, who, in spite of what had happened, was glad that we were doing well. Each successive dinner was more superb than the one before. Cec filled his pockets. The conversation often lapsed into periods of mute surprise that we could talk at all. Mitch kept his eyes on his plate. Glenn refrained from badgering John. The chair where Alan had sat remained as it had while he was there.

I remember, now, that he told me in the airport in Santiago, as we waited for the connecting flight down, that he came to these exotic places to fulfill an image he had of himself. As far as I'm concerned, it's much simpler than that. Life isn't a game. What you don't know can kill you.

Fish Story

When Robert Gardner discovered that his wife Jessie had slept with another man, he went behind the house and shot himself in the face with a deer rifle. Levert Gardner was born seven months later.

Jessie named him Levert for the uncle who raised her because her own father had left when she was three to hunt diamonds in South America. Levert died when a bear mauled him while he was cutting winter wood up in the Crazies, but only after he'd crawled half a mile with his stomach in his hands. Jessie was nineteen then, so they moved to Big Timber, where Robert got a job haying for the Tillotson Ranch and ran irrigation water along the Boulder River for anybody who would have him, because he loved fly fishing and wanted to guide for Dan Bailey's in Livingston, before he met Jessie, that is, and she slept with him.

Lev, he was called, right from the start. Jessie, nor her friends, nor anyone at school ever called him anything else. When he turned eight, he found the bamboo rod Robert had saved all that money to buy, before he met Jessie.

The rod was the color of creamed corn. When he found it in the attic of the old house they rented at the end of Fifth Street, he removed it from the leather case and held it to the light. There were words he couldn't read and a cork grip his fingers barely fit around, but he took it to Jessie, who was in the kitchen making bread.

"It was Robert's," she said. "He was nuts about fly fishing."

"It's broken," he said.

"No, it isn't. See? It's in two pieces, that's all."

She notched the tip to the butt section and waved her hand. The rod was a snake, darting back and forth. The color snapped against the soft light.

"How do you do it?" he said.

"I don't know," she replied. "It needs a reel and a line. He had those too."

"Can I have it?" he asked.

She thought a moment, her hands white with flour. A smudge of white was under her left eye. She shrugged.

"Why not? It's no use to me. But it was his, see, so don't hurt it. And don't put it together inside the house. Now, wash up."

A crazy man lived alone in a shack across the railroad line near the Yellowstone River. Everybody called him crazy, anyway, even Mrs. Stottlemyer, Lev's third grade teacher, who said it wasn't his fault, after all, he should be pitied, not tormented, the way the older boys did some times after school. It was said that the man, whose name was Jep, had been hurt in a mining accident near Billings, but others said he had been knocked unconscious with a wooden stool one night at the Ranger Bar in Harlowton and had been crazy ever since.

The first Tuesday of each month, however, he walked to the Citizens Bank to cash a government check that had four numbers in it, so there was money enough, people said, but nobody saw him around, not in the I.G.A or the state liquor store or even the Country Pride, where everyone went once in a while, for the chicken fried steak, mashed potatoes and string beans.

45

Lev saw him in the summer, when he rode his bike across the Yellowstone on the old Harlowton Road. There Jep would be, standing in the river, the water climbing his bare legs, nothing on but his underwear, a yellow wand like Robert's drifting back and forth, a long, thin line sailing above his head. Lev could not understand how such a thing might happen, so he stopped sometimes to watch, because the man liked to make the line go far out and return without touching the water. One time, late, just at sunset, after he'd had an argument with Jessie, he rode to the bridge, and Jep was there, buck naked, in the middle of the river, the line drifting away and back in a long, tight loop. He must be crazy, Lev thought, but he watched anyway, until the river and the darkness were one, and all he could see was that loop of line, high up, shining faintly in the last light.

Jessie was near thirty, now, and never remarried. She worked as a checker at the I.G.A. and sometimes at Dave's Sport Shop, while Shirley Ligas took care of her mother, who had Parkinson's disease. Dave had gray hair, a crew cut and wore a Colt 44 on his hip when he carried the moneybox to open the store in the morning. He tried to touch Jessie sometimes, though she never encouraged it and called him an old fool to his face. She smiled when she said it, though. Dave's wife Esther was in a nursing home most of the time.

Jessie went to the movies in Livingston sometimes with Wayne Carnehan, who cut meat at the I.G.A. and ran a few horses at the Tillotson Ranch. Sometimes Wayne was there at the house when Lev got home from school and always had candy bars he'd taken from the store. Wayne told him about his own boy, who was with his mother in Bozeman, and how he couldn't get along with him because of what she always said. Lev was glad Wayne never brought his son to Big Timber.

But Wayne was all right. He asked Lev to come along with Jessie and him when the cutting horses were in town. Sometimes they all walked to Winston's on a hot summer night and Wayne bought ice cream cones. Jessie laughed, though, when Wayne walked away from the house.

One day when Lev got home from school, a stranger was sitting at the kitchen table drinking one of the beers Jessie kept in the refrigerator. He was a small man with black hair and ferret eyes. His arms bulged under the white tee shirt. His neck was as wide as his head.

"You'd be Levert, then," the man said, in a voice like something scraped against rock.

Lev sat down opposite the man. He watched him drink the beer and smoke a cigarette. In a while Jessie came home. She went to the sink to wash her face. Then she said, "Lev, this is Milt Ashlock. He'll be staying awhile."

After dinner Jessie and Milt went upstairs. Lev did not see either of them again until the following day, when he got home from school and Milt was there, sitting at the kitchen table drinking beer and smoking.

That went on for a week. Then one night, when Milt was in the bathroom, Lev said, "Why is he here?"

"Mind your own business, now," she said.

"I don't like him," Lev said.

"That doesn't make any difference, now, does it?"

"I still don't like him."

"Don't you let me hear you say a word," she declared, smacking one hand against the other.

He closed his mouth. She ran her fingers through her hair, which was longer than it had been.

He said, "Did you know him from before?"

"From before what?"

She looked at him. Her face was expressionless, like Mrs. Stottlemyer's face when everyone was writing and she stood alone at the front of the room.

"Before," he said.

"I've known him a long time, if that's what you mean. He's just going through. He's got a job in North Dakota in a while. It's just on the way, that's all."

"What does he do?"

"He works. What is this?"

"I don't like him."

"It's none of your business, now, is it, Mister? And why should you notice if your mother is lonely sometimes? Your dinner's always on the table. Your clothes are always clean. Isn't that right?"

"I like Wayne."

"He's a fool," she said. "His hands stink."

"Is Milt my father?" Lev said.

"What?"

"My father."

She burst into laughter so loud that Milt rushed into the room holding his trousers with one hand and waving a cigarette with the other. "What the hell's going on?" he declared.

"He wants to know," she said. "He's wondering—." She shook her head and opened her mouth at the ceiling. "Are you his father?"

"Haw!" Milt bellowed. He fell to the sofa next to Jessie, waving his muscular arms. Lev saw the frayed line of his underwear. "If you was my kid, you'd have considerable more meat on those bones, and that's a fact."

Lev went down to the bridge.

Wayne didn't come around anymore, so one day after school, when Jessie had a day off and drove to Livingston with Milt, Lev went to the I.G.A. Wayne was cutting meat. His left eye was black. There was a long gash across one cheek. He didn't say a word, so Lev went home.

He was asleep when Jessie and Milt got back from Livingston. He woke when Jessie threw a beer glass at the kitchen sink. He crept to the head of the stairs.

"Settle down, my ass," he heard Jessie say. "You're as stupid as Robert. You'll never amount to a goddamn. Why do I always hook up with men who never amount to a goddamn?"

"I've got that job," Milt replied. "I told you I had it."

"You come by to blow your whistle," Jessie said. "So here I am again. You owe me twenty-five hundred from before."

"That's the job in Fargo," he said. "Come there with me. You'll get it, and more."

"I'm not going anywhere."

"You like it," Milt said. "You didn't forget any of it. You wanted it all, like before."

There was another crash, hollowness, a high-pitched squeal, as when someone's arm is pinched, a dull slap, then something hit the floor. Lev ran down the stairs and into the kitchen. Jessie lay on her back, her arms above her head.

"You sonofabitch," she cried.

Milt looked like something wild come down from the mountains. A sliver of blood was at the corner of his mouth. He kicked Jessie.

Lev flew at him, butting his head against Milt, striking with tiny hands. Milt picked him up by the hair and threw him against the wall. Jessie screamed. She was screaming when Lev crawled out of the kitchen. She screamed when Milt kicked her again. She screamed one last time when Lev brought the deer rifle in from the hall closet and fired it at Milt, striking him between the shoulder blades.

Pieces of something flew out the other side of Milt and struck the wall. Milt slammed against the kitchen cabinets, then dropped, swearing and hammering his fists. He caught Jessie high up on the face, shattering a cheekbone. Before he could swing again, Lev put the barrel of the rifle against Milt's head and pulled the trigger.

It took awhile for everything to calm down after that. When Jessie got out of the hospital and they went with Wayne to Winston's to have ice cream, Lev said later, "Then Robert wasn't my father."

"No," she replied.

So he took the rod case and walked to the shack on the Yellowstone River.

It was a small shack with one door and a window with no screen. The shack was overgrown by shrubs and vines. The paint was off the wood. Lev stood for a time. He could hear the river on down below. Then he tapped the gray door.

There was no answer, but something moved inside. He waited. The door opened.

The head of the crazy man came out. The face was unshaven. The hair was together in clumps. The nose was long and thin, like a beak. The brows were clumps of black, straight across. What Lev noticed most, however, was the eyes, as blue and bright as the porcelain vase on Mrs. Stottlemyer's desk.

"What is it?" the head asked, in a quiet, level voice.

"I'm Lev Gardner," he said. "I live in town. I have this." He held out the rod case.

The door opened a bit more. The man was not wearing a shirt. The skin was burnt copper. There was a patch of curly black hair right in the center of the chest.

The man's eyes went up and down the leather case. He closed the door. In a moment he came out wearing a tattered flannel shirt, faded jeans and tennis shoes. He took the case and removed the bamboo rod. His eyes opened a little. He ran his fingers up and down the clear, buttery varnish. He jointed the sections together, raised his arm. The rod dipped forward and back, glinting in the sun.

"You have a line?"

"I can't find it," he said.

The man now seemed smaller than before. He went into the shack and returned carrying a canvas pouch. There were round, fleece-lined cases inside the pouch. The man opened one and removed a gunmetal, perforated reel. Wound upon the reel was a thin, gray line.

The man fastened the reel to the rod. Carefully he strung the line through the guides. From his pocket he removed a coil of fine, almost transparent material and knotted it to the line. To that he tied a small, bushy thing that rested in the palm of his hand like a bug fallen from the trees.

He walked down through the cottonwoods behind the shack. Lev followed. There was a wide, flat place in the river. The man waded out. The water boiled against his thighs. He turned finally, facing the bank, where Lev stood watching.

Lev watched as the line went up and back slowly and came forward in a quick, tight loop. Each time it made a rhythmic turn, the line lengthened a bit, until there was more than enough to cover the distance from the back step at his house to where the lawn touched Fifth Street. Then there was a final push. The line darted forward, the tight curve unfolding and unfolding, until only the bushy thing at the end trailed behind, when everything went straight at last, settling the thing quietly to the surface of the river.

Lev smiled.

Almost immediately a bulge came under the bug, then an explosion, then something bright silver and green was in the air, throwing a jewelry of water and light. The man whooped. Lev grinned. After a time the man lifted the trout in both hands, the rod tucked under one arm.

"Three pounds, you can bet," he called, and slipped the trout into the water. At that moment Lev felt something he had never felt before.

The man waded ashore and walked up to the shack. He removed the reel and line and unjointed the rod. Carefully, he returned the rod to the leather case.

"It's good," he said. "You leave it here. Anytime you want, you come. I'll show you. You can use this reel."

Lev watched the man disappear into the shack.

"I'm Jep," the voice returned through the door.

Now, whenever he could, Lev was down there, learning from a crazy man. The man never talked much, but showed him how to cast, tie knots and handle the line on the water. When it got to where Lev didn't have to think so much, the man began to tell him about bugs, and he watched as the man fashioned imitations of them on a tiny, black vice.

Lev was amazed too at how this happened. The man had brutish hands, but the fingers turned delicately about wisps of feather and hair. From the jaws of the vice emerged creatures as fine as any he saw shimmering in the summer air.

"What are you doing in the afternoon now before I come home from work?" Jessie asked one day.

"Playing," he said.

"Playing where?"

"Around."

"Around the river, you mean."

She smoothed her hair, which was short again. He didn't say anything.

"I don't think it's right for you to be playing there by yourself. The river's fast and there are snakes."

"I'm not by myself."

"You're with your friends, then."

"Yes."

She slapped him.

"Mrs. Hamblin told me at the market how her boy Tony says you're down there with that crazy Jep learning to fly fish."

"He's teaching me about the rod."

"I want that rod back."

"I don't have it."

"Where is it, then?"

"I left it."

"You left it there? What do you mean, now, Mister?"

"He keeps it. I use his reel."

She sat down at the kitchen table so that she was at the same level as his head, but now she stood up.

"You're not going to turn out that way," she declared.

He said nothing.

"So I married him. So what. Sometimes you have to do things." She went over to the sink and looked out the window. "He wanted me awfully, didn't he? So I thought, maybe he'll turn around, want land, a few head of cattle, like Uncle Levert. But all he thought about was that fishing. Sat around mooning. You can't make a dime sitting around mooning, now, can you? You can't earn anything standing in a river."

She spun about.

"You won't be that way," she said. "I want you to amount to something. You bring that rod back, you here? That man can hurt you. He's crazy. Doesn't everybody say so? I'm sorry I hit you."

She sat down.

"You're too young to understand now, but you will one day. Make something of yourself. No man I hooked up with ever made anything of himself." She put her hands on his shoulders. "You're no dummy, Lev. All your teachers say so. You finish school. Get a diploma. Be something. You promise me."

He didn't say a word.

"Promise, goddamnit."

He nodded.

The next day he walked to the shack and asked for the rod. The man went inside and returned with the leather case, which he had polished. In his other hand he held the gun-metal reel.

"I don't have money," Lev said.

"I'm lending it," the man said. He put his hands in his pockets. "For as long as you need."

Lev stood awhile. The man stood too. Then Lev took the rod home and gave it to Jessie. Jessie put it into the hall closet. That summer Lev worked at the Tillotson ranch and at the Circle K. After awhile he took money to the shack and gave it to the man. The man said nothing but handed him a box of beautifully tied flies. Lev put it into his pocket. They stood for a while. Then Lev went home.

Sometimes when he rode his bicycle across the Yellowstone the man would be fishing in his underwear, the river climbing his legs, the fly line sailing tightly in a loop above the pearl green water, and he stopped to watch. He watched sometimes a half hour. Not once did the man look up, nor did Lev call down.

The next winter and one, when Lev was ten and halfway through the fifth grade, two men passed through Big Timber from Seattle and had the chicken fried steak at the Country Pride. They heard people joking about the crazy man who lived alone in a shack by the river, how he cashed checks with four numbers and never spent a dime. They waited until dark, went there and beat him for two hours. Then they killed him with a hammer, dumped his body into the Yellowstone and drove onto the interstate toward Billings. The body floated all the way to Greycliff before somebody found it. Lev went to the shack, removed the black vice and tying materials and hid them under his bed. The following morning the leather rod case was on the kitchen table.

The rest of the primary grades went fast. When he wasn't at school or working odd jobs, Lev was on the Boulder or the

Yellowstone, casting a long, gray line or turning over rocks and stones to examine bugs. In his room he created tiny flies from wisps of feather and hair. By the time he had finished the ninth grade, he had helped more than one fisherman from California, who bragged at the shops in Livingston about the kid from Big Timber who knew every hatch, read every riffle and current seam and got them into more trout than any four-hundred-dollar-a-day man with a McKenzie boat and a styrofoam chest of cold cuts and imported beer.

So Lev went to work for Dan Bailey's. He made enough money in the summers to give some to Jessie, who was well past thirty and seeing a different man every year. He got his diploma, third from the top of his class. Dan Bailey's offered him a job full time. He had saved enough money, though, and one morning caught the bus for Bozeman, a bag full of clothes in one hand, the leather rod case in the other. He left a note on the kitchen table saying, no, he wasn't crazy and would be back in a while.

The last time Jessie heard was a post card at Christmas. He was in New Zealand, fishing the Tongariro.

Something Happened

The bridge was there. He sat on a dead stump to rest.

It was an old suspension bridge. The girders were rusty. The metal plates along the bridge, however, were shining hot where the vehicles had passed. The road went over the ravine and into the trees.

He climbed down the hill, his boots making little puddles of needles and stones that scurried ahead, and walked out across the bridge to look at the river below.

The river was shining too, a band of aluminum flame, interrupted here and there by gray, bubbling ash. It was much too far. Besides, it was three o'clock, the bad time of the day, and he knew that his brother, who always quit early, would be waiting. Carefully he placed the upper part of his body over the rail and spat. Then he went on back to the Jeep.

Frank was sitting on a folding canvas stool eating a peanut butter sandwich, a clear, plastic cup of milk in the other hand.

"So," Frank said, when he came up. "How did you do?"

"A couple of 18-inch brownies and six or eight rainbows under that," he said. "You?"

"A few," which is what Frank always said when he hadn't done too well.

He wanted always to fish with his brother, and they started out that way every time, but quite soon he would look up and

Frank would be gone around a curve of the river or so far way that he could not shout to him over the tumbling water. It made him unhappy, but it was just as well. More than anything he loved fishing alone and listening to the high sound of the wind in the trees.

"Give me a sandwich," he said.

Frank opened the ice chest and drew out a plastic bag and a quart of milk.

"Don't drink out of the goddamned carton," Frank said, handing him a glass.

"Any more cigars?" he said.

"You brought plenty of cigars," Frank said.

He nodded and bit into the sandwich. The peanut butter was heavily smooth. He liked how it stuck to the roof of his mouth and how he had to make a clucking sound to get it loose or work it with his tongue, having the flavor go everywhere. He had liked peanut butter sandwiches from the beginning, when their father had taught them how to fish all that time ago. The old man was dead, though, and that was the name of that.

"So," Frank said. "What were you using?"

He put the carton to his lips, took a long swallow, bit into the sandwich. His mouth was thick with peanut butter. He enjoyed talking through it.

"Nymphs," he said.

"Nymphs," Frank said.

He nodded, watching his brother over the crust of the sandwich.

"What nymphs?" Frank said.

"Hare's ear," he replied. "I was using hare's ear." He smiled.

"What color?" Frank said.

"Dark," he said.

"Dark what?" Frank asked.

"Olive," he said, enjoying it. He had read four hundred books about fly-fishing.

"I was using tan. Maybe that was it, then. What size?"

"Eighteen," he said.

Frank shook his head. "I had on a fourteen."

"The water's pretty low and clear now," he went on. "They spook easily. Then I was using those yarn indicators I tie up. They land softly. Better. You know?"

Frank used the hollowed-out, fluorescent red balls clamped to the leader with a toothpick. They were easier to put on and to cast, but they splashed hard and looked like miniature barrels floating upon the surface of the river. Frank often was too lazy for his own good.

"There ought to be a caddis hatch this evening," he said. "We should get some good action."

Frank nodded, leaned back and closed his eyes.

The wind was in the tops of the pines. It moved an entire pine, stiffly, all the way down below the branches, so that the pine, moving, looked like one half of a great, wooden bow being pulled. Here, in the gully where they always parked the Jeep, there was no wind. It was warm in the sun. He ate, looking at his brother.

Frank was two years younger. His hair, grayer, was thinning at the crown, and he took naps in the afternoon. They had gone to Berkeley, gotten their degrees, gotten married and divorced. Frank had three kids. He had two. The kids were scattered about. Frank had a woman now, for quite some time. He had one too. Neither of them had remarried. They never talked about remarrying. They just never got married again and were both over fifty, and it was too late anyway, they never would remarry. It was the last thing their mother had spoken of, just before she died the season before, and they, the both of them, knew, without having to say a word to each other or to the old woman who had survived their father by twenty-five years, that they never should have married in the first place.

Frank was leaning back in the chair, his head against the door of the car. He thought about getting up and hiking down to fish the dark pools beneath the bridge, but it would be a tough climb getting there and tougher getting back. Then there was the hatch later when the sun would be behind the trees. He wanted to save himself. He had found that he could do everything as always, but it took longer to recover, and he had to save himself for what he really wanted to do. He couldn't do everything, but he could do what he really wanted, and what he saw in the mirror shaving each morning did not count.

He raised the lid of the ice chest and took out a Baby Ruth candy bar. Frank's mouth was open. It made a wheezy, wet sound. Frank would sleep now as long as he let him. He bit half way through the Baby Ruth. With the other hand he slammed down the lid of the ice chest.

Frank dropped forward, his eyes batting.

"I'll give you a few of those eighteens," he said. "I've got plenty tied up. We should fish nymphs before the hatch starts."

"All right," Frank said. "Sounds good."

"How about a cigar?" he asked.

"Why not?" Frank said.

He went around and opened the hatch of the Jeep. He had brought a handful of El Rey del Mundo from the humidor at home. He had a couple of hundred cigars cooking in the humidor. Bauza. Partagas. Padron. Aurora. El Rey del Mundo. He enjoyed acquiring knowledge of something and then using the knowledge. It didn't make any sense to go on with something and not know what you were doing. Frank smoked Chesterfield cigarettes and kept the few cigars he bought at the drugstore in a Tupperware bowl in the refrigerator.

59

He used a cutter to snip the ends of the cigars. He put one cigar into his mouth and handed the other to Frank. They sat in the shadow the pines made above the car smoking. "You want one of my indicators?" he asked.

"I'll stick with the corkies," Frank said.

"I tied another nymph off the bend of the hook, by the way. Midge pupa. Increases the chances."

"I'll try it," Frank said. "How far?"

"Sixteen inches."

Frank nodded, closed his eyes and puffed the cigar.

He looked at his brother. They had slept in the same room as children. Now here they were grown men, old men, and being a boy with Frank seemed strange and impossible.

"I put flowers on Mom's grave Tuesday," he said.

Frank, who lived in the Bay Area, did not say anything for a time. Then he said, "That's fine."

"They're keeping it up pretty nice," he said. "The grass and the leaves, I mean. They keep it clean."

A breath of smoke drifted above Frank's hat. Frank rolled the cigar in his mouth. "Fine," he said.

The old man's grave was on the other side of the cemetery, and he never visited it. He didn't know what Frank did. He didn't know if, after dropping him by his own place at the conclusion of a fishing trip, Frank ever stopped at the cemetery. It was a small thing anyway and didn't matter. He was sure that, after a time, he would not go regularly to their mother's grave. It was one of those things at first, which, after awhile, you just let go of. It was probably a good thing to let go.

"You want your Baby Ruth?" he asked. "I already had mine."

Frank dropped forward and pulled the cigar from his mouth.

"I expect I'd better," Frank said, "or it won't be there later."

"We still have those cookies Alison made," he grinned. "Too many of those for me to wolf down. You'll get your share."

Frank peeled back the wrapper of the candy bar and took a small, tentative bite.

"I don't see how you do that," he said. "I can't do it in less than two bites."

"That's easy," Frank said. "You're a hog."

"Hey," he said, "remember how, when we were kids, we'd put a whole loaf of that white bread away between us for dinner and a half gallon of milk. And still go out an play."

"I haven't got that appetite anymore," Frank said.

"Well, hell, I don't eat that way either, but I sure haven't lost the taste for it." He opened the ice chest and removed one of the cookies Alison had baked.

Frank stopped eating the Baby Ruth. The cigar went out.

He wondered, did Frank ever remember the silence of so many of those dinners so long ago? Their father had begun the affair when they were kids, and it had continued right on through their school years, including college, and even after they both had been married and had started families. He was the older and had seen what was happening and took his mother's side. Frank got what was left. It had not been planned. He just couldn't help it. He couldn't help hearing his mother cry or watching her face or seeing how she was. He couldn't help being afraid that she could leave and never come back. He didn't know if Frank was afraid too.

Now they were as old as their father had been when he died of the heart attack in that other woman's place twenty-five years before.

"Say, Frank," he said, "remember our trip to the Bighorn last August, just before Mom went?"

"What of it?" Frank said.

"We sure knocked them, didn't we?"

"It was a good trip," Frank said, relighting the cigar.

"Remember we floated down to that little island just below the put-in and they were rising right up along the bank and how Hale came by rowing those two fat guys from New York and kidded me about no fish being in there, it was too close, and then I nailed a big one right as the boat went by and they applauded, like it was a movie?"

"You and that competitive thing," Frank said.

He straightened, staring at his brother.

"What does that mean?" he said. "It was great, wasn't it? It was a real occasion."

"You want the rest of this Baby Ruth?" Frank replied, taking his rod down to retie the leader.

Later the sun was behind the trees. They stood on the flat ground above the bridge looking at the river. They did not fish the river below the bridge, where the light was low and the coming back, dark and arduous. They always fished here. The walking was easy, the riffles and runs, moderate and soft.

"A hare's ear," he said. "Right along the bottom. Until we see some surface action."

"And a pupa tied off the bend. Sixteen inches."

"Right," he said.

Frank smiled.

They fished that way for a time, waiting for the hatch. The sun went lower still. Then the caddis appeared, bobbing and ducking above the water. They entered the river. The rods began working, the pale lines sailing out, the tiny imitations drifting to the surface, where the trout took them savagely. The light faded, and though the fishing was good, as good as it ever was, a heaviness entered his heart. He left the water and sat down upon a large rock.

Something happened all those years ago, something terrible and lonely-making, when, finally, he told his father that time at the dinner table just what he thought about it, and his father went outside and his brother went with him. They had come up through that time and never talked about it. All the years and all the separation, and they came together only to fish, speaking about nothing but the rise of trout and the mystery of the one that got away.

He looked up.

Frank was gone around a bend in the river.

Oedipus In Montana

I stood in the shadow the cottonwood tree made against the house. It was a slat frame house, the kind built in the 30's and 40's. I lived in one as a boy. My house was white with a peaked, moss-colored roof. Harold Bromely's house was white too, when my brother Frank and I first started coming to Montana for the fly-fishing. Even then the color was so faded that the wood pushed through, gray and twisted, like hemp. Twelve years ago Harold found a palette of chartreuse paint at a Ben Franklin sidewalk sale in town. The house became a beacon under the Montana sun. Pilots used it as a turning point into the runway at the county airport beyond town. From the gravel road above, it seemed an exotic toad squatted against the heathery sweet grass and the dark leaves of the cotton-woods along the Boulder River, where we fished each summer. I wanted to fish now, upstream, against the riffles.

Gordon Harber, who owned the ranch above Harold's, played the harmonica. His breath tapped each hole, like a finger upon a keyboard. He played Amazing Grace, Shepherd from the Hills and finished with Nearer My God to Thee. The ladies squinted into the light, pulling at the sleeves of their print dresses. The men held straw hats and wiped their red faces with checker-board bandanas. It was late July. Harold had died the week before.

The reception was at the Senior Center in town. Paper cloths covered a pair of folding tables. A bowl of macaroni salad; a bowl of potato salad, thick with mayonnaise; cottage cheese and fruit cocktail; sliced ham and cheese sandwiches with the crust removed; wicker baskets, one with Fritos the other with chips; cartons of salsa and onion dip from the IGA; the aluminum coffee urn and Styrofoam cups at the far end, haloed by six of Mildred Brandstad's blueberry and raspberry pies, partitioned into wedges the size of the two fingers of a Cub Scout salute. It was agreed that Mildred made the best pies in the county. She made pies for most of the affairs at the Senior Center. Everyone craved a military salute from Mildred's pies. Just there, one elbow perched near the aluminum urn, Emma Bromely had stationed her wheelchair, powdery ghost face turned for a kiss, earpiece cocked for condolence, which she compelled by demanding, again and again, while the mourners gritted their teeth, "What did you say, dear? Say that again, won't you?"

The next morning, after a quick ham and eggs at the Frosty Freez on the east edge of town, we drove to the river at Gordon's place. We usually started at Harold's, where we had first obtained permission thirty years before. Later it was permission at Floyd's above Seven Mile Bridge, the Allison ranch on the West Boulder, Chester's spread back on the Boulder, where The Horse Whisperer was filmed, or the Webster ranch, which had a trout hole the size of an Olympic swimming pool.

We bounced down from the gravel county road. The screen door opened. We stopped.

Gordon was Harold's age. He leased his ranch now to a cattleman from Laurel, who ran Herefords in the south pasture. Gordon kept a few sheep. Some hogs were in the old log pens below the house. "For the grandchildren at school," he told us in a sandpapery voice, which suggested a lifetime of smoking, though not a cigarette, his son Dan informed us, had ever touched his lips. He pushed his head up from stooped shoulders. The clamps of his suspenders gleamed. His eighty years of labor could not keep his face from shining against the blue Montana sky.

"How was the winter, Gordon?" I asked.

"Much snow?" said Frank.

"Oh, can't complain," Gordon said. "Can't complain."

Gordon was very religious. We had never heard him swear, not a hell or a damn, and never a harsh word about anyone or anything. Even the death of his wife Mae, who was the only woman he had ever known, three years before had not touched the fundamental core of optimism and humility.

"And how are your families?" he asked. "All well, I hope." His grizzled face opened to show a mouth without teeth. His blue eyes, coated by a gelatinous gray, could barely see. I was frightened for the summer we would come and Gordon would be gone.

I looked at Frank. Both of us had been divorced for decades. Faith had driven off with our wives in the second car.

"Fine, fine," I said, my voice thickening. It would be an affront to goodness if Gordon Harber were not redeemed.

"We sure miss Harold, though" Frank said.

Gordon looked at us with old eyes.

We drove the Jeep to the river. I opened and closed the gates. It was a two-wheel track through meadow grass and cottonwoods. No one came down here except the family for a picnic or an odd spin fisherman from Billings or Livingston. We scared up a couple of whitetail deer. Frank parked near the stump where we always sat to pull on our waders and boots.

The river was clear and smooth in the channels. A bright riffle came down a long chute into a flat that spilled away into another riffle, fifty yards below. The boulders on the far side were gray and dusty after the spring runoff. I heard a splash. Then half way across an olive snout rose, sipping mayflies hatching beneath the white spray.

Those who do not fly fish for trout fail to understand the ardor for moving water, the tick of the nine foot rod, the clay-colored line sailing, the tiny imitation coming to rest, soundlessly, three feet above a widening rise. In a crowd or sitting for cocktails in an amber light to say something to someone or alone on a couch watching people move behind a rectangle of glass, bird chimes in a purse, the silver, red or green rush of traffic on the cross town, in flight from the wail of lovers, the lassitude of friends, the impatience of children who wonder why there is no more to say, I am in water waiting for trout.

We strung our rods, pulled on our waders and boots and adjusted our vests.

"A few are working here," Frank said. "I think I'll try for them."

There was plenty of room below, but I wanted to go up river.

"All right," I said. "I'll see you at the log hole."

Over the years we had given names to all the best spots.

He moved into the water, stepping gingerly between the stones. In this part on the Boulder, from Seven Mile Bridge to the Yellowstone, there was not a flat place anywhere. The stones were mossy and slick. You fought them and the current. They revealed your age. The further out you went, the more dangerous it was.

I watched my brother. He was a good caster. On the second try a trout rose. Frank struck. The rod dipped. The line cut taut through the flat, arching downstream. The rainbow came out, pink and wet-silver, the body curved into a half circle, back and forth, throwing sparks. Frank led the trout into the net. He measured the trout. He knew I was watching. He turned and cupped his hand. "Sixteen inches!" he yelled.

I raised my right thumb and headed up.

I don't keep score anymore or fret about landing trout. I don't lift them from the river. I've considered snipping the hook bend of my flies. Perhaps one day I'll simply stand under a tree and watch the river. It seems the silly yet logical end of letting go.

I walked the deer trail we always walked through the trees. The trail came to a side channel, which, this time of year, was usually dry. I picked my way across the dusty stones and stepped onto the other side.

I went up into the pasture, choked here by nettles and weed, and struck out through the grass. White-faced Herefords gaped at me with bovine emptiness. It is a good idea to talk to cattle when you are in their space, so I asked them how they were and how the winter had been. I went to the log hole and sat down. Part of the log was in the river. It made a back eddy, where, three years before, I had landed a twenty-inch brown. I thought he might return, but he never did. Maybe he swam down to the Yellowstone, since the water is wide and deep and he could finish his days unmolested.

The best part of the river below Seven Mile Bridge runs through Harold's ranch. I wanted to fish the pipe hole or the long, deep run below the house. It was another mile up. I had walked it many times. I could still walk it. I sat on the log looking upstream.

Harold's first wife was named Elizabeth Burns. That was before our time. Elizabeth loved horses as much as Harold loved horses. Harold and Elizabeth rode together all through these mountains. They rode horses up the West Boulder and up the East Boulder, where Kenneth, Harold's younger brother, still lived. They rode in the Memorial Day parade along Mc-

Leod Street that year when Harold was the grand marshal. One day, the other side of Seven Mile Bridge, a rattlesnake spooked her favorite horse Belle, and Elizabeth was thrown. She broke her neck against a rock.

A year later Harold went back and forth to Billings. Then Emma was with him. Emma taught piano in Billings. She had gone to the university and did not like horses. She never rode a horse. No one here could figure it, except maybe Harold was lonely and liked piano music, which was understandable, but that did not help about the horses. Elizabeth and Virgil were childhood sweethearts. Dan Harber, Gordon's son, told us about it one summer. The only Harold we ever knew was the Harold with Emma Carstairs, who had weak legs. After Harold stopped riding horses, Emma slowed to a walker. Now Emma and her wheelchair were alone in Harold's house, and we would have to talk to her.

Harold Bromely was the finest, sweetest, kindest, most good-hearted man we had ever met in Montana. When he laughed, his head went back, camped upon his narrow shoulders, then wobbled, like one of those heads on a stick on the dashboard of a car. I had to laugh. Both Frank and I laughed. One night, hiking back in the dark after fishing a caddis hatch at the pipe hole, we found Harold and Emma having steak for dinner. Harold's left fist was clamped about the handle of the fork. He sawed at the steak.

"You boys hungry?" he asked, his eyes gleaming.

"Say, Hare," I grinned, "that sure looks good."

"Here," he said. "Have a bite. Go on."

He sawed a piece. I put it into my mouth. It was like nothing else I had ever tasted.

Emma's eyes were tolerant.

"My god," I said.

Frank took a bite.

"Oh, man," he said.

Harold laughed.

"Tell you what," he said. "I'll pick out a steer this summer, feed him up all year for you. When you come next year, Sven at the market will slaughter him for you. We'll let him set up as long as you're here. Then, just before you leave, Sven will butcher and wrap him, and you can each have half, and you can eat Montana beef in California."

Frank and I looked at each other.

"Hare," I declared foolishly. "What can we say?"

"Say you'll do it," he laughed.

So we did. The beef was cut into steaks, roasts and hamburger. We put everything into the car that last morning, drove to Livingston for the dry ice and sped a thousand miles to get the beef to California and into our freezers. That was Harold Bromely.

Now Emma was in the house. It was Emma Carstairs's house. At the reception someone said she would not move into town and that maybe a woman might come out to stay with her. Finally, a lawyer from Chicago or a surgeon from Los Angeles would buy the place. No trespassing signs would go up. It would be over.

I left a note and headed upriver.

It was a tough slog. I had to stay in the water. The willows and scrub growth were too thick to walk the bank. Years ago I plowed along against the current slapping an attractor or grasshopper pattern behind the rocks and along the seams.

Question: what goes on four legs in the morning, two legs in the afternoon and three legs in the evening? Answer: I and my wading staff, struggling against the Boulder River, in Montana.

I reached the pipe hole and sat down to rest. Tonight—Frank snoring in the other bed at the Lazy J Motel—my legs would cramp, and, impaled, I would be thankful that I was not up to my waist in the push of white water.

The pipe emptied the pasture on the far side of the river. A riffle came down from above and made a turn against the bank under the pipe. Over the years a deep hole had formed. Big trout were there, plenty of rainbows and browns and some whitefish. Caddis hatched in the evening when conditions were right. Under the bank, below the spray from the pipe, trout were rising in a row.

I stayed for an hour. I landed three rainbows and two browns, none under fifteen inches. I wanted to go to the run below the house. I wanted to fish beneath the willows.

I made my way against the riffle until I reached the head gate that spilled part of the river into a trough that fed the ranch land below. Above the head gate down the bank to the river Harold had dumped old car bodies to curtail erosion. Pasture met the cottonwoods and willows. There was a two-wheel track where Harold had driven his pickup. When I saw the house through the trees, I got back into the river.

I fished to the run. It was good fishing. The gradient was shallow. The big rock was there in the middle of the river at the head of the run. I went up, got out and peered through the willows. The rear windows of the house were open. The sunlight was flat against the wire screens.

A few mayflies were coming off below the rock. They drifted, spinning aimlessly in the flat water, drying their wings. I changed flies.

The trout rose easily. I slackened the line. They spat the hook. I was compelled to land only a few. I fished for the better part of an hour and then stood to watch. The mayflies came. The trout took them languidly beneath the open sky.

Then I heard music. It came brokenly through the willows. It interrupted the current, skipping and sinking. I stepped out, set my fly rod against a limb and crept back through the trees.

Emma was playing the piano. She played beautifully. The notes moved along my skin. It was Chopin maybe. Maybe it was Liszt. No, it was Emma. Emma Carstairs was playing the piano. An adamantine stubbornness that life had not come on proper terms gave way before the melody in her soul. In a concert of solitude, Emma made music in Harold Bromley's house.

I shut my eyes. I thought of Gordon Harber, who would never be sad, since he knew that to be born is to lose everything. On his knees before eternity, he believed a promise he could not comprehend, that one day, far, far away, he would love again, forever, all that he had lost.

Light is no salvation. Emma Carstairs drained the refuge of waters. I wanted to be young and full of wonder. I wanted to find her alone in the meadows. I wanted to begin where everything begins, and I knew nothing of rivers or trout. In dreams anything is possible.

The One That Got Away

I took an arm. Frank took the other. We pulled the body out of the river. It lay on the bank running water, the face putty-gray, like something forgotten at the back of the refrigerator.

He was middle-aged and a fly fisherman too. Neoprene waders. Unscuffed, cleated boots. A fishing vest that was still new. A fancy cotton shirt with balloon, Velcro pockets. A Paisley neckerchief knotted around the throat. An expensive, waterproof watch strapped to the wrist. Straight out of the Orvis catalog and A River Runs Through It.

"Must've slipped," Frank suggested, "in the riffle above, hit his head, and the current brought him down to the pool."

"Hard to say," I replied, shrugging. "He's been dead awhile, though. This didn't just happen."

"What do you bet there's a pipe in one of those pockets," Frank said, trying to stay above it.

I pawed around. There was a pipe, a big meerschaum with a deeply carved bowl. It wasn't broken in.

"Jesus," Frank said. "Poor bastard. I hope he caught one before it happened." He glanced upriver. "What do you bet the rod's there at the bottom. Probably a five-weight Leonard with a Hardy reel."

"Graphite," I said.

"Naw," Frank said. "Bamboo. Pipe's the giveaway."

"You're right," I said.

"Poor, dumb bastard," Frank said.

We stood looking down. It was a broad face with thick sideburns and a high, hairless brow. A thin moustache was carved carefully beneath the nose, which appeared to be fractured. The eyes were set wide, coal black and distant, as though, at the moment of death, they had seen something irrevocable and true and followed it out of sight.

"Hey, we know this guy," Frank said, bending closer.

"I never saw him before," I said.

"Sure," Frank said. "He was in Dan Bailey's yesterday when we came in to buy our licenses. He was fingering the fly rods and wearing a plaid, Irish cap. There was a blonde."

"Big breasts," I replied.

"You're just horney. It's understandable."

"I remember the cap," I said. "I didn't see the face."

"Well, there it is," Frank said. "Deader that a whitefish."

We had been coming to Big Timber, Montana, every season for over twenty years without missing a summer. Big Timber is the county seat. The people are kind and friendly. We know ranchers up and down the Boulder River, where we throw our lines with the illusion that the sport is yet uncommercial and that solitude, peace and a sense of discovery still remain. Virtually no one shared what Frank and I had come to believe were our private waters. But there are guides now working the other side. And here was Mr. Orvis, flat on his back, and a river ran through him.

"We'd better tell Harold," I said, "and then the sheriff."

Harold Bromely, the octogenarian who owned the cattle ranch where we fished on this side of the river, was one of a kind and of the old breed whose fathers had homesteaded this part of Montana. Harold was set against the modern way. He would not drive in Billings because of the traffic lights. There were no lights in Big Timber and only a few stop signs. Harold's wife Emma was in a wheelchair. He was sad sometimes, with a terminal sadness. I loved Harold more than my own father.

"He'll think it's pretty silly," Frank said.

"A fella shouldn't take on more than he can chew," I replied. "That's what he'll say."

"No respect for dudes pretending to be cowboys."

"A man should know his limitations."

"That's Clint Eastwood," Frank said.

"Sure," I said. "Clint's like Harold."

"Clint's not at all like Harold," Frank said. "Clint owns a big ranch on Hat Creek and won't let anybody fish it. Clint's a Californian. Like this guy."

"You're kidding. How do you know?"

"I watched the blonde get into a silver Mercedes when they left the shop. It had a California plate. The guy was in the passenger seat."

"It's like that," I said, staring down at the dead man. "Amateur," I finished. But I was thinking about big breasts.

Later that evening, after we had eaten the chicken fried steak at Crazy Jane's, we sat out front of Room 12 at the Lazy J—where they had filmed The Horse Whisperer—smoked cigars, drank rum and Cokes and watched the storm clouds, which gather in the afternoon, blow down from Livingston. Larry Bradstead, who owns the Lazy J and is a California transplant, came out of the living quarters on the other side of the laundry room and sat down. He is a short guy with a baldhead and a red face from playing golf three times a week on the nine-hole course at the edge of town. He brought a small tray of ice cubes, topped off our glasses and poured himself a rum and Coke. He knew all about the dead man.

"He was a contractor from Palo Alto," Larry said. "Staying at The Grand. His wife's coming in tomorrow."

I looked at Frank. "Who told you that?" I said.

"The sheriff," Larry said, taking a pull on the drink.

"What was he doing on Harold's spread?" Frank asked.

"He wasn't at Harold's. He walked up from the access two miles below. The sheriff found the car there."

"Silver Mercedes," Frank said.

"How do you know that?" Larry said.

"We saw him," Frank said, "when we were in Livingston buying our licenses."

Larry nodded and leaned back in the chair. "Poor bastard," he said. "What's the good of money when you're that stupid?"

"He was stupid, all right," Frank said, looking at me.

"All by himself," I suggested.

"That was a mistake," Larry said. "You don't go scrambling around the Boulder alone. You fall and break a leg or some damned thing, you're in a world of hurt."

"Predator," Frank said.

"Arnold," I agreed.

"Actually, it was Jesse Ventura. That was his line."

"You're right," I said. "Jesse Ventura."

"What are you guys talking about?" Larry said.

"The movie," I said. "Predator. Arnold Schwarzenegger and Jesse Ventura. See, this lizard-like alien comes down from a space ship and is hunting Arnold and Jesse and their buddies in the jungle."

"Yeah," Frank said. "They went in there to rescue a combat team that had gone in earlier, and this lizard space alien, he..."

"You guys are nuts," Larry said. "Too much California. You ought to move up here, get away from that crap. Have a simple, uncomplicated life. Like me."

"We've talked about it," I said.

"Maybe we will," Frank said, winking at me, "now that everybody's foot loose and fancy free."

"What do you mean?" Larry asked.

"Never mind," I said. "Frank's blowing off again."

"Hand me that rum," Larry said.

We sat for a while watching the dark sky to the west. The wind shook the top of the pine trees in front of the motel. A guy in a straw hat drove by in a yellow pickup, honked, and we waved. We know a lot of people in Big Timber.

"His wife's coming in tomorrow," Larry repeated abstractly.

For a moment he seemed lost. I wanted to ask him about Sharon, his wife, whom he had returned to the sanitarium in Bozeman the summer before. We hadn't seen her since we arrived. I decided it wasn't a good thing to ask. This time, maybe, Sharon wasn't coming out.

"She's from Palo Alto?" Frank said, winking at me.

"That's what the sheriff said. She'll probably drive the car back."

"All that long way across the Nevada desert and thinking about her husband drowning in Montana."

Larry shrugged. "Maybe she'll arrange about the car."

"We know someone who'll drive it back," Frank smiled. I shook my head.

"One of you, I suppose," Larry said.

Frank shrugged. "Why not? Never driven a Mercedes."

"Besides," Larry said, "he never drowned."

"What do you mean, never drowned?" I asked.

"There was no water in his lungs."

Later we were propped up in the two queen-size beds. Frank was playing with the remote.

"She murdered him," Frank said, settling on the wrestling matches from Montreal.

"What a way to go," I said.

"She hit him on the head and dumped his body into the river. There was a lot of money involved."

A huge, muscle-bound ape had just slammed another muscle bound ape in black tights and a Batman mask to the canvas and was sitting on his head.

"And then she leaves the Mercedes there and walks all the way back to town swinging those big boobs and nobody even noticed. Right?"

Frank hit the remote. A black and white came on with Spencer Tracy and Katharine Hepburn. They were in love.

"Well, it's a theory. Maybe she and some cowboys up here are in it together. You never know."

"Sure," I said. "Maybe Harold himself."

Frank laughed. "Okay. But it sure seems funny. No water in the lungs."

"He hit his head on a rock and was dead before he went under."

"Arnold did it."

"Jesse."

"A guy might do anything for boobs like that."

"Boobs aren't everything," I said.

"Well, I'm a boobs man. You can have what's left. Frances had no boobs at all."

I thought of Joyce, my just-released wife, who had been quite fine in all the departments. I had expected to think of her. But I had thought that being up here would help with the feeling. It hadn't.

Frank must have been watching my face because, in the middle of a Spencer and Katharine kiss, he said, "Hey, you're better off. They get to owning you after awhile and you're done. You start asking permission and you're finished. You get guilty. Know what I mean?"

"Never apologize," I said. "It's a sign of weakness."

"Duke Wayne," Frank grinned.

"Yours truly," I replied.

Frank laughed. "You take me. Since Frances and I split three years ago, it's been better. A helluva lot better. Answer to nobody. Do my own thing. When and how."

"Lord of the mountain."

"King of the road. Go where I want to go. Fly rod in hand. And there's always somebody, if you need somebody that way. There's always somebody."

"All the way up to Montana from Menlo Park in a silver Mercedes. With an overnight in Reno."

"And in Winnemucca," Hank said.

"In Elko."

"Hell, in Jackpot. Screwing your way to Big Sky."

"While the missus stays home, faithfully cleaning, trimming the roses, devotedly waiting for the phone to ring at nine o'clock, which is ten o'clock here because it's Mountain Time."

"He had it all figured," Frank said. "Plenty left over for you know what."

"The right equipment. Rod. Boots. Vest. The best flies, hand tied at Dan Bailey's."

"Gold Ribbed Hare's Ear."

"Prince Nymph."

"Zug Bug."

"But a river ran through him."

"And dead men get no tail."

Frank shook his head.

"Stupid," he said. "You can't afford to be stupid. What good is all the stuff if you're going to be stupid?"

"And now Boobs is hiding out at The Grand."

"She had the hook in," Hank said, "but the big one got away."

"And now the sheriff has Boobs cornered, waiting for the missus to arrive to reclaim the body."

"The car," Frank said.

"Sure," I said. "The car."

"What will she do?" Frank said. "What will she say?"

"She's trapped," I said. "Like a fish out of water."

"The missus."

"Boobs."

"A standoff," Frank said. "Imagine their faces."

"I don't have to," I said. "I can see their faces."

Frank looked at me. "Forget it," he said.

"I can't," I said. "Crime doesn't pay."

"Pat O'Brien to Jimmy Cagney, before Jimmy fries," Frank said. "Hey, you'll get over it. It takes awhile. Everyone makes mistakes. Time heals all wounds."

"My mistake was stupid. You make stupid mistakes when you think you're being smart. Like that poor asshole in the river."

"We're all stupid, one way or another."

"I was really stupid. Stupid, stupid. I didn't even like her. I thought I was missing something. I was missing something, all right. Brains."

"What was that one's name?" Frank said.

"Lorraine," I replied.

"Stupid name."

"You're telling me."

"But Joyce was stupid too."

"Why?"

"For letting you go, over something so stupid."

"What are you talking about? Joyce was smart. She did the right thing. She was damned smart."

"But it's stupid to break up something that was all right just because somebody does something stupid. Life shouldn't happen like that. I explained it to Frances before we split."

"Catch and release," I said.

"In sickness and in health."

"Let him who is without a hook make the first cast."

"Till death do us part."

"Shut up," I said, "and watch the damned movie."

I love Spence Tracy. I love how he acts. I love his face, those interior, soft, vulnerable expressions around the eyes and mouth. Kate was happy to have him, no matter what he couldn't do, how guilty he felt or how much he drank. Poor Spence. He reminded me of my father, who had gone on with a woman all during my childhood and into manhood until the day he died. But my mother never let him go, no matter what. My mother and Kate. Till death do them part.

When the movie was done, I went outside and lit a cigar. Frank waited a bit, then came out too. I offered him a corona, and we sat smoking and looking at the stars. I didn't want to talk anymore about it and neither did Frank. We both sensed that we had reached a point where we should leave whatever had happened to privacy, since nobody ever figures it out, and stick to what we loved together, big trout and the high, star-beaten sky of Montana.

"Where, tomorrow?" I asked.

"West Boulder?"

Anna Wilson owned a big spread on the West Boulder Road. Her husband Sterling had died the year before, and now she lives alone on the ranch where she was born.

I know exactly what I'll do.

I'll fish upstream away from Frank, sit down on my favorite rock in the middle of the small, freestone river, plant my neoprene, boot-studded feet in the cold water and lay my rod across my knees. I don't need to go after those beautiful orange and yellow-spotted brutes the way I used to. Water does marvelous things when you only watch, and there is life along the banks and in the fields you never see without enough pain to make you sit still.

In the end it's best to live for one thing and let the rest go. But I wonder if, later, after Frank's gone to sleep, if I might just walk over to The Grand and knock at the door where a blonde with big boobs cowers in terror of a dead man's wife. Maybe she'll let me to drive her back to California.

Motel Man

The fire came over Ben Milligan's house. It took Ben's fly rods, melted his fly reels, consumed his fly tying materials and turned to ash every photograph he had taken of where he had been, what he had done and everyone he had known. It took the things Frieda had abandoned in the divorce and that he could not throw away. It took what his father and mother had left behind.

Ben moved into the Lewiston Valley Motel, which was the only place in town besides the Trinity Inn near the river, and that was more than the insurance company would allow. There were fifteen units in the motel, joined together under a common roof. The doors to the rooms created the appearance of closets that opened to the blacktop and the field beyond.

At first it was strange staying at the motel in the town where he had lived for forty years. The room had a double bed, a round mahogany veneer table with two vinyl chairs beneath a window next to the door, a small microwave and refrigerator and a TV upon the dresser below a mirror with a crack in one corner. There was an alcove with a washbasin and mirror, a Mr. Coffee that held four cups, a wicker basket with packages of regular and decaf, which were replenished each morning and which he could not open with his fingers and so tore at with his teeth. To the right was a door that opened to the toilet and tub shower. Towels were held to the wall above the toilet by wire rings. An extra roll of toilet paper sat upon the porcelain tank cover.

He took his meals at Mama's Place, which was eighty yards up across the macadam parking area and thirty yards from the mini mart that had the only gas pumps in town. It wasn't Mama's Place anymore because Oma and Dick had retired. Some people from Redding had the place two years now. They had renamed it The Lewiston Valley Grill, but it had always been Mama's Place. The same people in town worked there and Jim, Oma and Dick's boy, who stayed with them in the yellow house across the road because Dick had Alzheimer's and Oma was arthritic, still cooked relief sometimes in the afternoon.

At Mama's Ben sat at the counter, even though the booths were more comfortable and he could watch the deer that came down to the open field in the mornings and evenings.

"I was at the kitchen table drinking my third cup," Ben said to Patsy Erdman, whose husband Bill had been at the lumber mill for twenty years. "I looked up at Bear Back Ridge, which is in plain view from my house, you know, and there was the fire, rolling over the top, like lava that you see from those volcanoes on the History Channel."

Patsy wiped the counter and picked at the thumbnail she had broken moments before.

"I don't watch the History Channel much," she said.

"Well, that's the way it was, kind of liquid fire rolling off the mountain. It's what I get for living in the woods west of town."

Patsy shook her head. "You were lucky to get out of there, Ben."

"I suppose so," he said, studying Patsy's white, freckled arm as she refilled the cup. "I tried to wet down the roof and

84

the side of the house. What can you do with a garden hose and no pressure to speak of?"

"Nothing," Patsy said. "You were damned lucky just to get out with your skin. It took Bev and Phil Beckwith's house too, did you hear? They lost everything. And no insurance." She shook her head.

"Where are they now?" Ben asked.

"At her sister's in Klamath Falls." She wiped the counter. "How about you, Ben? You got insurance?"

"I'm seeing him later," Ben said.

"You're lucky, then," Patsy said. "We haven't got insurance either. How can we afford insurance?" She looked at Ben and tried to smile. "So how do you like it at the motel?"

Ben thought about it. "I don't really know," he said. "It's weird, so small and nothing your own."

"Are you sleeping all right, Ben?"

"Oh, sure," he said. "Never any problems with sleeping, but I don't like the damned light coming in over the curtain and the work crews up when its still dark and starting their damned trucks. But I suppose that's part of it."

"I can't get used to the burnt smell," Patsy said. "If I leave the windows open, it's awful. If I close the windows, I sweat. But what can you do, right?"

Ben shrugged. "It will go away in time," he said. "What we need is a good rain."

"Fat chance. It's already June," said Patsy. "I hate looking at the burnt timber whenever I go back there."

"That will take longer," Ben said. "A lot longer."

"What can you do?" said Patsy. "You're lucky you have insurance."

She went to the till. Her hand was shaking.

In the motel Ben sat on the double bed looking at the blank TV. He thought about Frieda. They had split the year before, and he had not heard from her. That was okay, he supposed, since the parting had been particularly bitter. They had lived together there in the house for so long, he couldn't help wondering how she would react to seeing everything but the chimney charred flat to the ground. There would be a twinge about it, certainly, and he would have liked to see her face. A home was something you did together. But now it was gone, Frieda was gone and everything he owned was gone, so there he was, sitting upon a double bed in the Lewiston Valley Motel staring at an empty TV. How could you make sense out of that?

There was a knock at the door. In two steps Ben's hand was on the knob.

"Mr. Milligan," the small man at the threshold said. "Howard Atkinson. I'm the adjuster with American Insurance. How are you, Mr. Milligan?"

Atkinson wore brown flannel pants that hung short above scuffed wing tipped shoes. He wore a white short-sleeved polyester shirt and a clip on tie, the clamps of which shone dully in the hot light because Atkinson had unbuttoned his collar. He held a clipboard and a yellow sheaf of papers.

Atkinson came into the room and sat in one of the vinyl chairs under the window. Ben left the door open. It felt good to have the day inside along with Mr. Atkinson. Ben sat upon the bed.

"I've been out to have another look, Mr. Milligan." Atkinson made a clucking sound. "A terrible shame. Terrible. Terrible. Were you able to save anything at all?"

"Nothing," Ben said. "I had to get out of there. The fire came down like an eruption." He wanted to tell about the History Channel.

"It must have been something," Atkinson said, arranging the yellow sheets of paper upon the table.

Ben thought a moment. "It was," he said. "All I have is the truck."

"Parked out front?" Atkinson said.

"That's it," said Ben. "I had the keys in my pocket. I jumped in and drove right out of there. I suppose I was lucky."

"You were that, Mr. Milligan. You were, indeed. And even after such a tragedy, you are lucky still. You have American Insurance on your side, Mr. Milligan. We'll put everything in order, just as it was. It will take a little time to get started, of course. There's the paper work. There are bids and such. New codes and ordinances since your house was built. These things happen. But we'll take care of everything. We should be able to get started in, say, six to eight weeks. How are you fixed? Are you comfortable here? Do you need anything?"

Ben looked about the tiny room. A smoke detector was fastened to the ceiling above the bed. Every twenty seconds it blinked red. He had been long enough at breakfast for new towels to be brought in. The Mr. Coffee carafe was clean. Fresh bronze cellophane packages were in the wicker basket.

"I'm all right," Ben replied. He shrugged. "What else can I say?"

Atkinson nodded. He had been through it many times before and decided that he did not want to say again what he usually said.

"I'll leave some papers with you," Atkinson said, standing. He took out his wallet and produced a card. "Look them over. Call me if you have any questions or need anything." He stepped to the door. "I'll be talking to you about the features for the house. We can make it just as it was or you can have some modifications, if you like, a bigger living room area or kitchen, perhaps. Cosmetic things here or there. As long as we stay within the original square footage and use similar materials. You understand, I'm sure."

Ben nodded. Atkinson went out into the sunlight. "Of course," he remembered, "If you should decide not to re-build, we can issue you a check for the market value of the place. It is all pretty much burned around there. You might not want to see all that from a new house. Some people just want to get out." He nodded. "Something more to think about, I know."

Atkinson waved, climbed into his car and drove off.

Ben stood in the doorway. He looked at the field where the deer came down. He looked at Mama's Place. There were only a couple of SUV's out front. It was an hour before lunch. He looked at the mini-mart, where a tourist was filling the tank of a ski boat.

After lunch he drove out to have a look. He hadn't gone out since the fire. He had not wanted to go out. He saw it in his mind. He heard the flames and smelled the smell. When he got there, that's how it was.

The earth was burnt and charred. There were a few metal rungs and pipes, like black, broken bones. The stubs of burnt cedars stood around. If some of the cedars had trunks or branches, the trunks were black, and the branches were black sticks stuck into the trunks. There was the smell of everything black and burnt and dead.

He did not go to where the house had stood. He had seen on television how people after a fire picked through the embers, looking for something, anything. He stood by the truck. He looked at where everything had been. He closed his eyes and imagined the house, the pine needles upon the shingled roof, the chimney and the wisp of smoke, all the cedars around and deer coming down, heading for the meadow beyond. He even imagined Frieda hanging clothes on the white parachute cord he had strung between two trees. He opened his eyes. He got into the truck and drove to the motel.

The room was gloomy, so he used the metal push rod to shove back the curtain. He went to the bed and sat down. He got up to look out the window. There was a Jeep parked at Mama's Place. It had a trailer with a couple of dirt bikes. At the minimart a man a man was putting gas into the tank of his motor home. A calico cat padded across the parking lot and into the field. The sun was hot on the blacktop. He went to the bed and sat down.

He got up and opened the door. It was pleasant with the day inside the room. A fly buzzed in, hurried about and left.

Ben took one of the vinyl chairs from the table and set it beside the door outside. He closed the door, lit a cigarette and sat down. At the end of the motel to the left, the blacktop rose to a grassy plateau beneath cedar and jack pines. Trailer homes were parked there. Wires and hoses came out of the trailers. On top of the trailers were satellite dishes and radio antennas. The trailers had painted names, like Montana or Mountain Eagle or Sundowner. There were hookups for a dozen trailers. A half dozen were there now. Bob rented the spaces for as long as anyone wanted.

Around the corner of the motel to the left and out of sight was a public storage that Bob also owned. It was the only storage in Lewiston. Before he sold it, Ben had kept his own boat there.

He thought about the boat now. Then he thought about fishing. It would be good to go down to the river above the bridge and fly fish for trout. The flow from the dam was at 350 cubic feet per second, perfect for putting a fly below white riffles and the seams beneath the willows. His fly rods and reels, his flies, his fishing vest, his waders and boots, everything was gone under the fire. He'd have to go over to Herb Burton's shop and begin collecting gear again.

He sat in the shade outside the motel.

He had the retirement, the social security and what his parents had left at the bank in Redding. He had the money from American Insurance. He did not know how much Bob was charging American Insurance. Bob dealt directly with the company. But he didn't owe anybody anything. No one owed him anything. He looked at the empty field.

He didn't want to go over to Herb's. He didn't want to browse through all the things, picking and choosing. He didn't want to talk about the fire and go over it with everyone he met.

He decided to drive to Elmer Burrows' place to borrow a rod and reel and use Elmer's old waders and boots. Elmer and he were the same size. Sometimes, if one of them forgot something or something was leaking or broken, they shared. He put the chair into the room, closed the door and drove to Elmer's.

Elmer did small engine repair and lived in a trailer near the river. Ben borrowed the fiberglass rod, the dented Pflueger reel and Elmer's patched waders and boots. Elmer gave him a dozen flies in a plastic cup covered with tin foil. Ben drove to the road and crossed the bridge. He turned down the dirt trail to the parking area Fish and Game had prepared the year before.

The river was low and clear, the rocks mossy and brown. The riffles sparkled in the light. The river came out of the top of the spillway a few hundred yards upstream. It came down, bubbling, frothy and white. A fisherman was below the spillway in the first riffle. Ben saw the glint off the fly rod as the man's arm came back and went forward.

Ben put on the waders and boots. He knotted a size eighteen tan caddis downwing to the tippet of a nine-foot leader. He stepped into the water.

The water was a rising shock. It was strange not having his gear around him. He had tied thousands of flies. He always carried twelve or fifteen boxes of flies to the river. He liked carrying a lot of flies. He felt proud and professional carrying so many flies. Now he had the dozen Elmer Burrows had tied. He was wearing Elmer's patched waders and Elmer's old boots with the broken laces. He was using Elmer's fiberglass rod, which was stiff and unresponsive compared to the Winston graphites he had collected over the years. But that was all right. After a bit he found a rhythm. He began to catch trout. He caught big trout. He had a dozen flies. He lost the downwing caddis and four or five other flies, but at the end of the afternoon he had released enough trout to give him complete satisfaction. The fire was out of his mind.

He returned Elmer's gear and drove to the motel. He left the door open and sat down upon the bed. In his shirt pocket was the plastic cup with the flies he had not used.

He put the cup upon the round table beneath the window. He moved the cup to the dresser and sat down. Bob walked by on the way to the laundry room. Bob waved through the door. Ben put the cup into the refrigerator.

He walked over to Mama's Place, sat at the counter and ordered the chicken fried steak with white gravy. The Redding paper was on the counter. He thumbed through it, but he wasn't interested in reading.

Ellen Burmeister came in and sat down beside him.

"Well, hello there, Ben," she said. "I haven't seen you for awhile."

"I suppose that's so," Ben replied. "Even in Lewiston folks sometimes miss each other."

"They do, don't they?" Ellen said. "That's so."

Ellen Burmeister was a slender and still attractive woman, thin faced, with round blue eyes that effervesced when she was excited. She was Frieda's age. Frieda and Ellen were friends. Ben had wondered what Frieda had said during the break-up. There was plenty to talk about, since Eddie, Ellen's husband, was so mean that Ellen had wanted to leave too. But then Eddie was diagnosed with pancreatic cancer. He took eight months to die.

The chicken fried steak arrived. Ellen ordered a bowl of chili and French bread. They sat eating.

"It's awful about the fire, Ben," Ellen said.

Ben nodded, chewing.

"Were you able to save anything at all?"

"Nope," Ben said. "Not a thing."

Ellen shook her head.

"How awful! Have you told Frieda?

"I haven't talked to Frieda," he said.

"Funny," she said. "I haven't either."

The door opened. Four out-of-town fly fishermen came in. They wore khaki shorts with cargo pockets, vented shirts with button-up sleeves and baseball caps with logos of trout and the names of outfitters. They sat down in a booth under a window.

"What will you do?" Ellen said, breaking a piece of bread and dipping it into the chili.

"I don't know that," Ben said.

"I understand," she said.

He finished the chicken fried steak. Ellen finished the chili.

"Like to split a piece of lemon meringue pie?" Ellen smiled.

"Sure," he said. "Why not?"

They ordered the pie to be cut for two plates and ordered two cups of decaf. They sat eating the pie.

When the pie was gone, they ordered two refills of decaf. They sat drinking.

"It's early," Ben said. "I think I'll watch the six o'clock news. Would you like to finish the coffee and watch with me?"

"All right, Ben," she said.

They walked down to the motel. Ben unlocked the door. He moved the vinyl chairs from under the round table and set them next to each other at the side of the bed. He left the door open.

They watched the news and finished the coffee. Ben made a carafe of decaf, tearing at the bronze wrapper with his teeth. They drank two more cups. Then the news was over.

"Do you want to watch anymore?" he asked

"I don't think so," she said.

He switched off the TV.

Outside, in the twilight, the deer had come down to the dusty field. He pointed. She turned to look.

"Isn't it sweet," Ellen said. "They're almost pets, aren't they?"

"Maybe they should have names," Ben said.

"No one has even given them names," said Ellen.

Ben sat down. "That's probably a good thing," he said.

"Why do you say that?" she asked.

He thought a moment. Then he said, "They don't belong to anybody."

They sat a moment. Ellen said, "Would you ever like to come over for dinner some evening, Ben? You always did favor my pork roast."

"All right," he said.

She looked at her hands. "I should be out of that house, I know. It's acceptable now, if that makes any sense. You have to live somewhere."

Ben shrugged.

"Saturday night?" She stood up.

"Sure," he said.

The next day he went fishing. He had only the flies in the refrigerator, but they were enough. He caught a dozen trout, climbed out of the river, lit a cigarette and sat down under a willow tree.

The river was very clear and bright. Midstream, behind a rock, a trout rose. It rose again. He thought about getting out there to catch it, but he sat beneath the tree smoking.

There were red and green patches on both legs of the waders. One of the bootlaces had broken again. He had had to tie the boot at the top. The boot squirted water when he stepped onto the bank. Upstream an angler was playing a trout. He saw a splash and a silver gleam. The gleam disappeared into the water. The rod bowed and throbbed.

Ben sat watching the water. It was better than yesterday. He was in no hurry. It did not matter when he got back to the motel. He liked fishing with a few flies. He liked fishing with a borrowed rod and tackle. He looked up. A black and white eagle sat perched at the very top of a jack pine. Its yellow beak was hooked and sharply pointed. The eagle was also watching the water. The eagle turned its head. Its eyes never left the water. The trout rose behind the rock. The eagle flung itself down. At the last moment it spread its wings, splashed bluntly into the water behind the rock, its claws stretched and hooked. It rose, the trout pinched, spewing water like a sponge. The eagle flew off down river, the trout curving and uncurving its tail.

He had seen eagles catch trout many times on Hat Creek, which was fifty miles the other side of Redding. He loved Hat Creek. The water was clear, clean and smooth, like bath water. Maybe I'll fish Hat tomorrow, he thought. He stood, crossed the river, the cold rising above his thighs, removed the waders and boots and drove to Elmer Burrows' mobile home.

"Hell, Ben, why don't you just keep the damned things? I don't use them anymore. They just sit around here. Keep them. Go on."

Ben laid the waders and boots upon the workbench Elmer had made from scrap lumber.

"Elm," he said, "I couldn't do that. No place to put anything. I'll come by when I need them, if that's okay." He leaned the rod against the mobile home.

Elmer shook his head, "Suit yourself, Ben."

"I will take a few more flies," he said. "Might go over to Hat. I'll need some pale morning duns and a few blue wing olives. Nymphs too."

"Must be great being retired," Elmer mumbled.

At the motel he unlocked the door but left it open. He set one of the vinyl chairs outside and lit a cigarette. He looked at the sunset against the roof of Mama's Place. There was one car at the side away from the main entrance, Patsy Erdman's '78 Camarro. That meant Jim had walked across the road from Oma and Dick's to cook. He felt sorry about Oma and Dick.

He sat smoking and watching the sky above the jack pines beyond the field.

There was nothing to do, no obligation, no future piling up in the corners. He felt young and fiercely strange and wondered if, approached in the right way, Bob might cut him a deal to have the room on a long-term basis.

O, Brother!

My brother and I go back to the beginning. This is both an oxymoron and a revelatory truth.

I'll explain.

Frank's birthday is today. I bought him a ceramic coffee mug. Inscribed on the mug is Happy 70th. You're old. Get over it.

That's not the only thing I got him, of course. We have our jokes. Inside the mug is a gift certificate from L.L. Bean. We're fly fishermen. Bean has fly fishing stuff.

I'm seventeen months older that Frank. That means I got to use the car first. I went off to college first. Like that. Our mother had just the two of us. Pop's been dead over forty years. Mom died on Mother's Day, it's the truth, two years ago. We're what's left, not to exclude the kids, of course, and the grandkids on Frank's side. Mom did my birthday in October and Frank's in March. It was all family for Mom. Frank and I wanted to keep it going. Frank lives in the Bay Area. I live in the Central Valley. Now it's March. Frank is seventy today.

We meet for lunch at Spenger's, a Berkeley seafood grotto that goes back farther than Frank and I do. Pop took us there when we were kids. A corporate chain owns it now, but it's the same outside, and Grandma Spenger still lives upstairs. The bar's the same and the teak wheel in the middle of the room, the chairs between the spokes. We corner the wheel. Frank brings his girlfriend. I bring mine. Whatever kids can attend, come. Frank has three. I have two. This time, however, it's only me. My son has to work. My daughter is in Seattle. She never comes. Susan, my friend, is busy.

So I drove over.

We sit around the wheel. It's been only a couple years, but already there's a pattern. We don't order lunch. We order appetizers, plates of appetizers. We order beer and wine. We share. It's a common meal. We dip our fingers and eat. It must have been what the ancestors on Mom's side did in Lebanon.

Seventy years. What's to say? We talk about fly fishing. We plan our trips to Montana and Idaho. We've gone to Alaska, Canada, New Zealand and Chile. It's what we do. Fly-fishing. That's the oxymoron.

Let me explain.

Pop was a fly fisherman. He taught us in the high Sierra, when hardly anyone was doing it. Campsites along the Mokelumne. Up as the crack of dawn, down river with the two fly dropper system. Black gnat on the bottom. Royal coachman on top. No one fishes that way anymore. We fished that way. We spread the trout we caught upon a coarse, woolen blanket. I have the photographs. They were in Mom's hall closet.

Nothing mattered when you were ten years old and had the dropper swing. I wasn't learning anything from Frank. What was Frank was learning from me? Everything was big, outside, certainly, but big, and all we wanted was to go there and live where everything was.

Then you're seventy.

Revelation.

I'll explain.

Who else do you spend a childhood with? Who else survives that time but a brother? There wouldn't be any wife. Not even a girlfriend. There's just a brother. You sleep in the same room. You eat the same food. You see the same thing. You go to the same places. Your parents drive. You're in the rear seat. A bond forms, deeper than blood. You listen. Even with a seventeen-month lead, everywhere you are, there he is too, your brother, like an extra brain or heart. It's the foundation for understanding. The years pile on. You're seventeen months ahead. What can you say? Maybe something happened or you did something. But he's not where you are. He's there, of course, but he's never going to catch up.

That's the illusion.

That's the oxymoron.

So Frank is seventy, sitting beside me between two spokes of an enormous wheel, only now, who can tell the difference? We're gray-haired old men. His children and grandchildren are here. They surround him, like petals on a wooden flower. I kid him about Viagra. He kids me about Lipitor. We order the appetizers.

"So I'm tying plenty of grasshoppers for the Boulder," I offered.

"Good," he replied, looking at me out of the corner of his eyes. "It's going to be another drought year in Montana. We'll need plenty of grasshoppers."

"Sure knocked them last year, though, didn't we, Frank? The ol' hopper with a dropper."

He frowned and plunged his fingers into the calamari. "You and that damned competition. What if you did get the biggest rainbow? I got the biggest brown."

"Unverified, though," I said. "Definitely, unverified."

"You were downstream."

"Well," I laughed. "What's with the competition thing? I take your word for it. Just clean fun. They'll be bigger this year. You watch."

"Ever the optimist," Frank said.

Something drops in me, like a rope bridge between rock walls. I struggle to be a twin, but how can there be equilibrium, not with that seventeen-month lead, which asserts itself subtly, temperamentally, at any time, with no choice on my part. It makes the entire room push away. It leaves me with my fingers in the calamari, alone in the desert.

Candace, his girlfriend, sits to his left. She is busy with control, passing the plates as they arrive, seeing to the drinks. She's not like his ex-wife, but she is, if you know what I mean. There's that thin, hard edge behind the eyes whenever she doesn't get her way. Frank has made my mistake.

But my divorce was first, naturally. Frank said, with my house in the country and my kids in the private school where their mother taught kindergarten, "I thought you had it made."

The competitive thing.

I didn't have it made, of course, but the remark told me that things between Marian and Frank were tenuous. Then he had the affair, which, in a reflex of guilt—a carryover of our Catholic upbringing—he confessed to her one bleak night in winter. Marian got hysterical. He called me. I drove over on the interstate and practiced a kind of brotherly therapy, from the vantage point of seventeen months. Marian was furious. Frank wept. I pointed this out to Marian. She was mollified. They reconciled. Frank looked at me gratefully through shining eyes. I gasped. I felt something there, out there, from the one person who had been around from the beginning. Had Frank come up to speed?

No luck. Six months later they were divorced. I was where I was, and Frank was over there, specifically and metaphysically.

So much for a foundation of understanding.

Frank opened his presents. He tore at the wrapping paper. He yanked at the ribbons. The floor was littered. Crap piled upon the wheel in front of him. He shoved the shrimp and calamari aside.

A collapsible wading staff. Shirts from Nordstrom. A landing net. Polypropylene socks. A baseball cap that said Trout Bum. A box of See's chocolates. Three dozen lottery tickets from Curtis, his son, who was a house painter. A digital camera from Candace. Books. A blue sweat suit from Candace (sweat suits are all he wears now. "They're comfortable," he declares. Is this a concession to time?). A gift certificate from a restaurant in Santa Cruz, where his daughter lives. My coffee mug, which says, You're old. Get over it.

He had it to himself. No shoving from me under a Christmas tree. No waiting his turn behind seventeen months. It was delightful. I sat back. I watched. It was Frank. It was Frank's goddamn birthday, one day out of the year. It was Frank's seventieth birthday. I crossed my arms. It was funny. This was my family, my extended family, to be exact. I include Candace. Frank and Candace have been together more than twenty-five years, more than Frank had been with Marian. She doesn't go back to the desert, of course. No black hair. No black eyes. But what the hell? Aren't we all ancestors, digging our fingers into life? One big, happy family?

That's the oxymoron.

The waitperson brought the desert tray. She was the same waitperson who had done my celebration seven months before. Her name was Ginger. So we called her Ginger. We looked at the chocolate, caramel and cream-filled things arranged in a circle. I didn't want desert. Desert had plugged the arteries. But it was Frank's birthday, for chrissake.

Candace ordered one of everything.

Fate intervenes.

We drank coffee and put our forks into the deserts Ginger brought. The deserts went around the table like edible jewels. I took my share.

When Mom was alive, we had these parties at her place, a small, two-bedroom house we rented for her on Poplar Street. She always made more than one desert. Pumpkin pie and chocolate cake and brown sugar fudge. There was a lazy Susan. We sat around and dipped our fingers. Mixed nuts, M&M's, potato chips, York mints, caramel chews wrapped in cellophane. She made raviolis and fried chicken. She always had a bowl of green beans. We called her Green Beans. She got old. Then we went out for dinner. Chinese. Indian. Mexican. But she always managed desert and the lazy Susan. We'd go back to her place after the Chinese or whatever. It was timeless. She was ninety-six when she died. I found her, legs crossed, lying on the dining room floor in an eternal nap. I carried her into the bedroom and called 911, just before Frank arrived from the Bay Area. We stood together looking down at Mom before they took her away. "We'll be closer now than ever," I said. He agreed.

That was Mother's Day, two years ago.

Why is everything a life story?

So we sang. Ginger brought over some of her waitperson buddies. They stood above Frank. Everybody sang.

"Happy birthday to you. 'Happy birthday to you. Happy birthday, dear Franky. Happy birthday to you."

Ginger had a vanilla cupcake with a candle. Frank blew it out. Ginger filled the glasses with champagne. We finished the deserts, down to the last crumb.

Then it was over. We sat around wondering what to do. Candace went outside for a cigarette. Frank and I paid the bill. I had a couple of cigars. I gave one to Frank.

We strolled up the street from Spenger's. The women looked into the shops. We sat outside a coffee shop and puffed.

"I hope the water isn't too low on the Boulder, though," I said.

"Just low enough for hoppers," Frank replied.

"I'll have them all ready," I said.

"That's good," said Frank. "We'll need them."

There it is.

Your brother sleeps in the same room with you. He eats the same food. He sees and hears the same things. Your world is his world, but only, it seems, in some arcane, historical way. The same events occur, but they're not recorded in the same way.

A lot of my friends are leaving too, who, if they don't go back to those first days, have been around long enough for me to have learned something. Their names appear in the paper. I'm experiencing not so much a mourning as an odd resentment that they have slipped away, and I did not know them. But your brother is your brother. There is no other brother.

That's the oxymoron.

That's the revelation.

When is a story a story and not a commentary? The containment of time by drama is necessary if we are to live, but what holds the narrative together is hidden irrevocably by a seventeen-month lead.

Life does not imitate art.

All the trout in the world, behind dark stones at the bottom of the stream, don't mean a thing, if you can't go there and breathe. Caged, with eyeholes and a mouth to eat, you spend your days alone feeding and end up starved.

It's enough to make you believe you have a soul.

"So, what do you say, Frank?"

"About what?" he replied.

The girls were coming up the street. The Berkeley air was crisp and clean and smelled of the sea. I clapped him on the shoulder and stood up.

"Oh, nothing," I laughed. "It's time to go."

He is my brother. It is foolish to expect anything more. Don't misunderstand. I am not a fatalist. But I refuse to dust the furniture.

I'm first. That's the way it is. Still, I would give anything I own to know what my brother will think, looking for me on that last day.

Fisherman

We were sitting in the cabin having a drink after that first morning's fishing when Bill ran in to tell us there was a dead man out in the wood.

"A dead man," Tom said.

"He's under some leaves," Bill said, pointing, and hurried to the counter to pour himself a drink.

We looked at each other, waiting for something else. Bill's hand was trembling around the glass so we stood up.

We went outside. Bill led the way through the aspen trees. There was a small space, about the size of a picnic table. A few leaves were thrown back. A man's legs came out of the leaves.

"Jesus," Henry said.

"I stumbled over him cutting through from the stream," said Bill. "Scared the hell out of me."

We stood looking down. Tom's face was white. The dead man's trousers were stretched like sausage casings, and a sweet, molding scent filled the air. We stepped back.

"I wonder what happened?" Henry asked.

"A heart attack or maybe an accident," Bill said. "Maybe he fell and broke his neck. I almost broke mine running to the cabin."

I kicked more leaves off the body. "So they just left him here," I said.

The man wore a green and black plaid shirt and a green felt hat into the band of which was stuck an assortment of artificial flies. He was a fisherman like us.

In the eyes of each of my friends I saw the same awareness. We had been brought to a remote area of the north wood and set down near wild lakes and streams for a week of marvelous sport. The only way in or out was by plane. Urban men, stifled by the press of twentieth century life, hunger for such things.

"What are you saying here?" Henry asked.

"I'm not saying anything, Hen. Just giving information."

"Jake, are you suggesting this guy was maybe killed or something?"

"I'm saying that people don't come out to these places alone. That's what I'm saying."

"All right, so what would some guy be doing out here by himself?"

"Precisely."

"So he wasn't alone."

"They fly guys in here all the time, don't they?" Bill said.

"We had to have reservations," I replied.

"So the guy comes in with some of his buddies, he has an accident, breaks his neck and his friends fly off without him."

"How does that sound to you?" I said.

"You think something happened, then," Henry said.

"I don't know what happened. But he was left behind. That happened."

"His friends couldn't find him, maybe," Henry said. "He got hurt out here and they couldn't find him. So the plane took them back and there'll be search parties." He looked at the sky.

"Maybe his friends caused the accident and then left him out here for somebody else to find so it would look like he wandered away or something."

This speech of Bill's seemed to bother Tom, and he went off to stand alone.

"Why would friends go and leave you like that, if it was an accident, I mean?" Henry said.

"They wouldn't," I said.

"Maybe they didn't want the notice," Bill said. "They didn't want to be involved in all the notoriety."

"Some friends," I said.

Tom returned and we stood looking at the dead man.

"Well, what are we going to do now?" Bill asked. "We just arrived and we have a whole week with this guy lying out here."

"We'll have to bury him," I said.

We fished in the afternoon and did the best we could, but that night we hunched over our steak and beans and said nothing. When Henry, who, on the strength of his biscuits, was always nominated cook, brought forth a steaming batch from the reflector oven, I wanted to be cheerful.

"I lost a monster today," I said. "Sonofabitch must have been two feet long. Came out of the water, shook its head and broke me right off."

The others only nodded, so I bit into a biscuit.

"I guess there's no way we can call out, then," Henry said. "I mean there's no radio around here or anything."

"That's what we wanted, remember?"

"I was thinking the same thing," Bill said.

"What's the matter with you two?"

"If we had a radio, we could leave. It's creepy. A dead guy we buried in the woods. How are we supposed to sleep with a dead guy out there that somebody maybe murdered?"

"I'm going to sleep," I said.

"You could sleep through anything," Bill said. "You're a rock."

"We're stuck, that's all," Henry said.

"Stuck?" I replied.

"We have a whole week to get through."

"I don't believe this. Tom?"

Tom stood up. He went to the door.

The air in the tiny cabin was stifling. The shadows made by the fire crawled through the bunks against the wall. Henry's biscuits were doughy. I left mine half-eaten and followed Tom outside.

I have been a few places, packing on the Tahoe-Yosemite trail, for example, or camping along the Yellowstone River in Montana, where the stars are so bright and clean you'd swear they just came out of a dishwasher, yet they stay where they belong. But here, two hundred miles from anywhere, in the deep north wood, the night is different. There is no distance between earth and sky. Darkness fills the trees, and the stars are silver flames scattered among the limbs.

I did not see Tom at first. Then there was a movement, just where the clearing fell into the wood.

"So here you are," I said.

He grunted and looked off through the night. There was no sound, not even the whisper of wind through the trees.

"What do you make of it?" I asked.

"What do you mean?"

"Do you feel the way Bill and Henry do?"

"I don't know," he said.

"Seems silly to me."

"Oh, it's not silly," he replied.

"I don't mean about the dead guy."

"I know what you mean."

I stood quite close to Tom. Our shoulders almost touched. "It's not as though we ran out of gas," I said, "in the middle of nowhere and had to find a station. This is not even on the way. It's something you read about in a newspaper. I'm not a bastard because I want to catch ten-pound trout after burying a corpse we found in the wood. We've been planning this trip all year."

"You're right, of course," he said. "It just takes you by surprise, that's all."

"And it's not a question of being heartless or cold or anything like that. You can't take things out of context, Tom."

I felt him move beside me.

"I've always admired that about you, Jake. How things don't get out of context."

"They get to me."

"Well, but you're in charge. They don't get you down."

I didn't like what he was saying. I know that I seem to have this manner about me. People call me an optimist, when there's every reason to think otherwise. It's true that I try to build something positive out of what happens, but, for all I know, this may be cowardice, even if my friends perceive it as courage.

"We have a whole week up here, Tom. Are we going fishing or aren't we?"

"Sure we are."

"Really fishing."

"I'm here to catch the big one, Jake, just like you." "What about Henry and Bill?"

"Don't be too hard on them. They'll come around."

"I'm not so sure."

"They're all right. Go on to bed."

"How about you?"

"What do you mean?"

"Aren't you coming?"

"Sure." He patted my shoulder. "Go on."

I walked to the cabin and climbed into my bunk. Henry and Bill were sitting at the table. I didn't say anything and went right to sleep.

The following morning we walked to the stream. It was an easy walk through the trees and across a small meadow. The stream was very clear and white blue and you couldn't see it from the cabin and the sound of it only came faintly at sunset. As soon as I stood on the bank looking in, everything left me.

We were all skilled fly fishermen and had decided, while sitting around the dinner table at home, that since we were going out so far, we should stick close together, but it has always been my style to wander off. Henry and Bill stepped into the riffle about thirty yards apart and their flies began touching the surface of the water. Tom and I walked upstream, where the faster water tailed out of a long pool, and Tom said, "Looks good."

"I'll go a bit farther up," I said.

The stream made a bend at the head of the pool. I walked up there and turned around. Tom's line was gliding upon the still water. I disappeared from view and decided to go up another quarter of a mile. There, quite alone, up to my hips in the cold stream, surrounded by tall pines, gray stones and clean, blue sky, I unhooked my fly from the cork grip and began playing line out over the bright water.

There is no way for me to describe the meaning of this. I had decided years ago to release every trout I caught. Except for an occasional meal—and this comprised only of those fish about the size of an ear of corn—everything was returned. The hooks were barbless. The captives were slowly worked back and forth in the current to regain their strength. Not even a trophy size battler was kept. There was something so primitive, so sure and true about this that I came to dislike intensely the period of history in which I lived.

I was never so alive, never so healthy and right as when I stood alone in a high mountain stream and struggled to land a large trout. The nature of the thing, that was what held me fast, the way earth holds the roots of trees. If I was getting older, if life was leaking away, out here I was timeless.

I worked my way upstream, netting a dozen big trout and losing as many more. The sun crept slowly to the tops of the pines. I was getting hungry, but none of my friends had come into view, and I grew suspicious again of the fisherman in the wood. I sat down on a rock and waited. I waited twenty minutes. Then I pushed the fly into the cork handle above the reel and headed downstream.

When I reached the pool where I had left Tom, I found it deserted. A hundred yards farther and there was no sign of Bill or Henry. By this time my stomach was showing symptoms of fatigue, and I surmised they had beaten me to the salami and onion sandwiches, so I made for the cabin.

Henry and Bill were seated at the table. Bill was cutting the bread.

"Where's Tom?" he asked. "We'll have lunch ready here in a minute."

"I thought he was with you," I said.

"You guys went off together."

"I went on ahead. He never caught up."

Bill put the knife down. "Maybe he circled around you and went on farther. We didn't see him come back down."

"What time is it?" I asked.

"A little after one," Henry said.

"Hell, he's still fishing, then. He's not been much of an eater lately."

I sat down and put a piece of salami into my mouth. There was a wedge of white cheese on some waxed paper and I cut a piece of that and sliced the onion.

"What is it?" I said.

"I don't like it," Bill said.

"Don't like what?"

"We were supposed to stick together. We're off in the middle of nowhere, and we said we'd stick together."

"He must have gone around me, then."

"Without letting you know?"

"It wouldn't be the first time."

"I don't like it," Bill said.

I made a sandwich and sat eating. After a minute Henry stood up.

"I think we should go check," he said.

Bill said, "Me too."

I looked at them over the top of my sandwich.

"He's got me worried anyway," Henry said.

"What do you mean?" I asked. "Worried about what?"

"He won't say. And now this appetite thing." Henry shook his head.

"He never said anything to me about anything."

"Naturally, he wouldn't, Jake."

I put the sandwich down and went to the door.

"All right, I'll go upstream," I said and left.

I was still hungry but another feeling was in my stomach, and I recalled a connecting flight that time in San Francisco and having the plane land just as my next flight was taking off and the feeling and that's what happens when you rely on someone and there you are, stranded and on your own.

I didn't want to be angry. Maybe Tom was hurt, though that seemed unlikely. It was being put upon more than anything else. It was being affected by the anxiety of others.

But even without the fishing, I found myself becoming grateful to Henry and Bill. The day was beautiful. The forest was deep and still. Now I could pay attention to the very shimmering of the leaves, the quickening of the stream around boulder and root. Fly-fishing was only an instrument of participation in something more permanent and real than anything man could provide. I moved upstream with a light and expectant heart.

I went a mile and a half and stopped. Surely Tom wouldn't have come this far. There were many good pools and runs and the fishing so fine that one could have spent the entire day on water no longer than a city block. He wouldn't have turned downstream, since he was a purist dry fly fisher. I sat down on a rock and lit my pipe.

It was then that a new feeling touched the back of my neck. I did not want to acknowledge it. I looked at the blue stream before me. I concentrated on the sound of the current. The feeling crept down my neck between my shoulder blades and touched the base of my spine. I stood up.

I walked downstream to where Bill had been fishing the previous morning and then cut into the trees toward the cabin. I came to the place where Bill had stumbled. Tom was there. He was sitting on the ground just where we had buried the dead man. He was sitting with his legs out and the leaves all around and he was crying.

I stepped back. My hands shook. I turned and hurried toward the stream. When I reached the cabin, Bill and Henry were waiting outside.

"Well, did you see him?" Bill asked. "There was no sign of him downstream."

I went by them and into the cabin.

"Jake, did you see Tom?" Bill said.

"He's back there," I said. "He's all right. He's fishing. I told you he was fishing."

"Well, then, did you tell him lunch was set?"

"He wants to fish. He'll be in when he's ready."

I got into my waders and put on my vest.

"You haven't finished your lunch," Bill said. "Aren't you hungry?"

I picked up my rod.

"Hey, Jake, don't be that way. We're a bit jumpy, that's all. And then to have a friend like Tom start seeing a doctor, you worry, don't you?"

"I'm going fishing," I replied. "That's what we're out here for, isn't it?"

Pale Morning Dun

That evening we crawled under the fence and looked at the house where old man Fario had died. Wooden slats were nailed over the windows and the front door was padlocked. The grass was brown like the weeds along the road. Some of the branches were dead on the willow tree.

"What do you think?" I asked.

Jerry looked at me and smiled. "No problem." He found a stick, broke it in half, put one piece between his teeth and handed me the other. We slithered forward on our bellies like Chuck Norris in the movie playing at the Bijou in Livingston.

We got across the dead grass, past the willow tree and Jerry held up a hand. I stopped, bit down on the combat knife, my ear cocked against the sounds of the jungle.

"What is it?" I said.

"I heard something."

The wind came up from the meadow where the stream ran. It lifted the American flag old man Fario always kept poking from the house. The stripes rolled, turned over and fell limp, like a wide red and white fly line. Something in the roof creaked.

The house had stood out here for as long as anyone could remember. The somber grey, which you see painted on a lot of the old places, was gone, the wood, slivered and bleached. Two pillars held up a portico which arched over the front steps. In the late afternoon, with the sun behind the cottonwood trees, it looked like the entrance to a cave or the deep, dark water beneath an undercut bank. Over the years, coming up from the stream along the dirt road toward home, we had seen a figure, wavering there in the gloom.

We were curious about him. Because he never went to town, never, as far as anyone knew, even left the house—food medicine and an occasional shirt or pair of boots drifting in to him from the stores along Front Street—he was mysterious and untouchable.

Now he was gone, disappeared to that deeper mystery, about which few ever spoke, even on Sunday, to which our own Grandpa Alan had gone one evening last year while Jerry and I were knee deep in Horseman's Run. Gramp loved to flyfish, even when his eyes got so bad he couldn't see the tiny imitation riding the crest of Horseman's Run, and Gram had to stand just out of his casting arc to tell him when to strike. He taught Jerry and me all we knew about trout, the patient, gentle rhythm of flycasting and the faithfulness of releasing everything we caught. The evening after Gramp disappeared I fully expected he would come in from the hill where he went to watch the sunset and take his place next to my mother.

We studied the house, hunkered down in the dry grass and weeds. We had no idea why anyone would board up the windows and fasten a lock to the front door of such a lonely place, unless it was to keep us out. This was, of course, the thinking of boys, who believe that life coincides with their passage upon the current of time, for hadn't we often hidden our rods and crept about the perimeter of the house, hatching a plan of attack, but prepared always for flight?

"I don't hear anything," I said.

There were underground storage rooms. We had observed the old man remove the chain, throw open the heavy wooden door, descend invisible steps and vanish beneath the house. It was then that we were at our boldest, crawling up to peer over into the emptiness and gloom. We never saw him. But we heard him—scrapings and grindings and the thick sound of things being moved, and his voice, low and muttering. We were amused that, deep down in the dark, the old man talked to himself.

We made our way round to the side, the odd calls from the jungle, the grotesque shapes of dying trees, the ashen fortress itself rising above us more dangerous than anything Chuck Norris faced, far back in enemy territory.

The cellar door was locked. Jerry grabbed the rusted chain and shook it. From the hollow below a sound returned, met itself, fell back, returned again. Jerry struck the door. The sound came with a growl, collapsed, mounted the stairs, moaned against the heavy wood, disappeared.

"There's no way in," I said, "c'mon."

"Maybe we could climb up," Jerry said, pointing to the second story. "Maybe there's a window or something."

"And maybe this isn't such a good idea after all. They don't want anybody around here, Jer."

"Who doesn't? Mom says there aren't any relatives. They can't find anybody to do the funeral."

"Well, somebody put up the boards and those locks."

"The sheriff, probably."

An older brother is an ambiguous thing. He goes first and shows the way, but he also charts paths into trouble.

"I don't know," I said.

"Well, what would Chuck do?"

I grinned. "Fall back and reconnoiter?"

He punched my arm and stood up. "We've been doing that for years. C'mon."

116

We had never seen the back of the house. It was concealed from the road, which dropped off sharply to the stream, and by the time we got up and by, a stand of cottonwoods blocked the view. The decay was worse. Spring rains always revived the front yard with wild flowers and sent out occasional shoots below the willow branches which had died the summer before, so that coming along the road, we found even the dark place beneath the portico less forbidding. But here the ground had been scraped so that not a blade of grass grew. Broken pieces of machinery were strewn about, rusted into the earth like iron bones. Beneath the rear windows were stacks of packing crates, their ends split open, boxes of electric motors, broken appliances and power tools: he had earned money by fixing things. There was only one door and it too was locked.

"Goddamnit," Jerry said.

A few paces from the back door was a firepit. I went over to have a look while Jerry studied the house for a way in. Around the pit were a few charred embers, bits of blackened metal and glass. A rusty gas can sat next to the pit on a block of wood. I kicked at the ashes. Something turned over and caught my eye. I picked it up. It was a perfectly white shirt button of a kind I'd seen all my life. The center holes where the thread goes were broken.

"Hey, Tom," Jerry called.

He was stacking some of the smaller boxes on top of one of the crates.

"That screen up there," he said, "I don't think it's fastened. C'mon."

The light had begun to fade. The air was getting damp. The dust we had kicked up hovered above the ground. Beyond, in the trees that obscured the house from the road, shadows pressed together. The edge of things was gone. It was the time when sound does not rise but spreads, like voices across a stream, yet there was no sound, not the slightest murmur, even from far away. I looked at Jerry. He floated upon the dust, hands on hips, watching me. I looked back into the trees. A bell had come down over us.

"Mom will be fixing dinner," I said. "We'd better get in."

"We'll tell her the afternoon hatch was late and they were rising like crazy. She won't care. Help me here."

We made a pile of rubbish on the crate and Jerry kneed his way to the top. He squatted a moment, then stood slowly erect.

"There's a piece of rope in that box by the door," he said, "grab it."

When I returned, he had already lifted the screen and was raising the window.

"Wait a second," I said, "Jerry," but his legs vanished over the sill. It was a full five minutes before I saw him again. I knew what he was doing. Sometimes on the stream I'd look back and he'd be around a bend fishing on his own. He didn't care anything about how I felt when I expected to find him and he wasn't there.

Then his head came out. "Wait'll you see this," he said. "Throw me the rope. I'll help you."

I shimmied up the house and dropped inside. It was a small, square room like a bedroom, but it was bare, not a stick of furniture, not even a rug. A door led into a hallway. Jerry went through and I followed.

The other rooms upstairs were empty too. The bathrooms had no towels or soap or anything to make you think they were used. "What'd I tell you," Jerry said.

We crept down the stairs. There was a large, open space that looked right at the front door. Through the dirty windows on either side I could just see the fence where the road was.

"It's filthy in here," I said.

Dust was on the tables and chairs, the curtains and lamps. When you took a step, a pillow of grey rose from the floor.

There were no pictures on the walls, no photographs on the counters, none of that stuff people have strewn around. We went through all the rooms and all the rooms were the same. It was as though someone had not lived there but only floated about.

"Let's go, " I said. "This is creepy."

"But where'd he sleep?" Jerry asked.

In the kitchen the sinktop was bare, not a glass or a cup. A door was at the far end. Jerry went over and opened it.

It was a small room, like a porch. Inside was a stool and a cushion in which there was a deep impression. Before the stool was a brass telescope, shining softly in the fading light. Certainly the old man had some consolation, then, for the house stood above the most beautiful place in the world. Another door was off to one side and Jerry tried the knob.

"Locked," he said. "Must be the cellar. I'd sure like to get down there. I wonder if it's the same. He was always shoving stuff around."

I was looking through the telescope. Beyond the cottonwood trees lay the valley of my boyhood. In broad, green swells it rose toward the arrowhead peaks of the mountains. I felt a softness for the old man. A heart that regarded such things could not be dark. I lowered the telescope. A narrow passage had been cut below through the shrubs and limbs. I could see right down to the slick patch of grey and the black arms of the big oak that hung above the water. I stepped back and the stool went to the floor. I pointed. Jerry hurried over and squinted through the lens.

"Jesus," he said. "Horseman's Run."

It seemed that everyone turned out to bury him, as many as turned out for my grandfather's funeral. Mom was forgiving, so Jerry and I went to the stream.

We like to get there before the sun touches the water. Everything is clean and new and fresh, the stones are damp, the air is crisp and clear, the cottonwoods stand green against the sky, the river comes down like blue steel, thudding against the rocks, frayed white over the marbled bottom.

I know now what flyfishing means, but even then Gramp had taught us to observe. "Don't jump into the water right away, boys," he would say. "Look first, and look right in front of you, against the bank. That's where the big ones lie."

We crept forward, half bent over, our rods behind us. We knew the river as well as we knew our own bedroom. Just here the stream swept round a curve, dropped through a riffle, then opened into a still, dark pool. Below that was Horseman's Run.

"Trout feed ninety percent of the time beneath the surface, boys," Gramp had said. "If you want to catch a lot of fish and big ones, weight your nymphs and bounce them right along the bottom."

He had taught us how to rig up, how to cast, lift the rod and concentrate on the leader for the slightest hesitation. We had watched him create the dark-bodied bugs that were so effective, for Gramp had studied the river for years. He even taught us how to tie the killer nymphs ourselves, but it was the duns that fascinated us.

"Those nymphs crawl around down there a whole year," he had said, "before they swim to the surface, break out of their skins and float along drying their wings. They live only a day more, and that's not long, is it, boys, to be so beautiful."

When Gramp tied those thin-bodied ephemerella, as he called them, on size-18 hooks, their pale green bodies and diaphanous grey wings reminded us of tiny, unmoored sailboats, and when the duns themselves were adrift upon the surface of the pool, we watched as an entire armada of delicate, translucent ships spun and took flight.

That's when the trout came up, finning easily in the slack currents, their snouts tap-tapping the surface as they took the duns one by one. It was the best time to flyfish. Everything was there. It was what Jerry and I loved. It was what Gramp, in the end, could no longer see.

"It's still a bit early for the hatch," Jerry said, kneeling in the wet grass above the stream. "Let's put on some nymphs and go down after them."

We rigged up and spread out. I made a couple of false casts and dropped my brown nymph just above the shoulder of a big rock. When the leader skipped sideways, I lifted the rod.

My arm came alive, the weight of the fish throbbed in my hand, the line ran past me and a 17-inch rainbow shot out of the water, curving and uncurving, wet-silver and pink. "Fish on!" I yelled, the rainbow coming down, shaking its head, the leader popping like thread, everything going slack and no weight. "Lost him," I called, but Jerry was stumbling along the bank, his rod arched dangerously, the line cutting a scratch across the steel blue water. The fish jumped twice. I watched as Jerry did all the things Gramp had shown us. Finally he removed the barbless hook, looked at me and smiled. I raised my fist. It beat anything Chuck Norris could do.

We fished like that for an hour or so. The sun went to the tops of the trees. The shadows flattened over the river. The air grew warmer and the dampness left.

"Look!" Jerry shouted.

Sure enough, in the heavy water above were tiny grey sails sculling down to the pool below. I couldn't fish right away. I never can when the duns first come up. I have to watch them, suddenly upon the surface, their wings drying for that one day of life above the stream.

"It's impossible to imitate them truly," Gramp would say, holding one up so that the light shone around the veins in the wings and filled the pale olive body. "Thank god we don't have to, or else we would be obliged to find some way to use them to catch fish, and I don't think we could do that, do you, boys?"

I did not understand then what he meant, but I knew he liked to watch the sails too, and I would find him sometimes standing alone smoking his pipe and staring out over the water. He was the smartest man I ever knew, and it was right to fool trout with delicate imitations. What a surprise it must be to lift up for something so easy to obtain, only to find the sting in your own mouth. It was good then to remove the hook, hold the fish in the current until it recovered and let it go, so that it sank down in a remorse that spared a few duns overhead.

I looked over at Jerry, who was busy snipping away the nymph and knotting on a dry fly. Circles had begun to form beneath some of the sails, and the sails disappeared.

The swish-swish of Jerry's line went out over the water and the size-18 dun imitation fluttered to the surface directly above a widening ring. The fly drifted, Jerry mended the line, a dark snout showed, the fly vanished, Jerry lifted the rod and a trout the size of my arm came out of the water and raced downstream. Jerry stumbled and laughed, trying to keep up. A thrill went through me. The duns don't understand or the trout. But everything is caught. Everything is let go. Everything is perfect. Nothing in the whole world is so grand as flyfishing.

I tied on my imitation, and for two hours Jerry and I worked the long pool and the riffle that dropped toward Horseman's Run. Then we sat on the bank, our feet in the water, and looked up at the sky.

"Chuck doesn't have this," he said.

"No way," I agreed. "There aren't any trout streams in jungles."

He looked downstream to where the big oak hung over the current. "Let's do the Run. It's still good. There will be a few duns. We can find a rise or two."

I looked at the deep, curling water. It was water hard to wade, unbroken at the surface, but heavy and swift. Lunkers held at the bottom and rose to the duns in the eddies and slicks. The biggest trout were in Horseman's Run.

"You think we should?" I asked.

"Sure, why not?"

I shrugged, looking up past the oak to the tangle of brush and limbs.

We stepped down, hunched over into our stalk. A circle formed near the bank just below the point where shadow met light. Jerry went to his knees, inched forward, his rod bowed back and forth, the line whispered above my head, the fly settled to the water, spun a little, caught a seam, then disappeared. In a couple of minutes he had landed and released a nice rainbow, scanned the water and then crawled down to another rise.

I watched, creeping along behind. We came under the black oak. The few duns that drifted on the Run seemed abandoned and lost. The fishing was tougher, and that was all right, that's how we liked it. I kept looking up through the branches and brush. There was nothing, but I couldn't fish. I just stared up through the jungle of limbs. I knew we were there, floating in the center of the lens.

All through high school and into college, when Jerry and I went away, the old house remained boarded up. We never tried to get inside again, and I was surprised when my brother lost interest in our most dangerous scheme, to sneak down into old man Fario's cellar. There were two reasons. Chuck Norris left the Bijou in Livingston, and Jerry discovered that Alison Sharp, who lived two houses up the road, was actually a girl. However, as the days passed, I still could not help stopping a moment each time we walked by, and after awhile, Jerry, ever more impatient, went along, leaving me to stand alone before that monument to age and decay.

It seemed finally to have stopped changing and to have taken on a timeless ruin. The walls, beams and columns were at last uniform with whatever weather might do. The roof stopped curling. The space beneath the portico grew permanently dim. Even the willow trees found neutrality between leaving and staying, the dead branches as appropriate as those which had managed to live. The house came to inhabit space, much like a large stone or the dark oak above Horseman's Run. After awhile it was just there.

But something did change. Though he went first, my brother and I had always been two faces of one thing. We did everything together, our dreams and hopes, our failures and accomplishments occurring with remarkable consistency. But with Alison Sharp along, Jerry seemed to lose interest in fly fishing, about which, Gramp had said, there was always more to learn. I found it hard to believe he could drift away like that, but, more often than not, I went to the stream to stalk trout alone.

At first this was intimidating. Jerry and I had a system. When the fishing got tough, we tried different imitations and methods until one of us found something that worked. Now I was left to figure out everything myself, and sometimes, when I cast for hours over water that contained fish, I felt confused and betrayed. Later, when I walked up the road past the old house, I could not stop. I could not even look. Something was there, wavering in the gloom beneath the portico.

But the most remarkable thing happened. I asked Jerry to go fishing with me one morning, which was the only time I had a chance at him because Alison was a late sleeper. He said, sure, we got everything together, even talked strategy, but she called and said she was going shopping with her parents in Livingston, wouldn't he like to come too. And he said, yes, can you believe it, so the next morning I got up before everyone, fixed myself a sandwich and went down to the stream while it was still dark. I was mad, madder than I'd ever been, and I sat on a rock to wait because it was so early I couldn't see the water.

I calmed down after awhile, ate my sandwich, the sky got a little white above the far hills, and that's when it happened. A shiver ran up my back. I felt him standing behind me, there in the trees, smoking his pipe, his fly rod leaning against a stump. He was waiting too for the sun to come over the steel blue water. And his voice said, "Be patient. Sit and watch. Don't always be in a hurry."

The sky grew lighter. The surface of the stream appeared beneath a soft glow. I heard a splash, then another. Trout were rising, but I couldn't see them. Then the color of the current separated from the dark, far bank. More splashes, but now I could see, and there was nothing, no duns, nothing, but the splashes were everywhere, the trout were feeding, but on something I couldn't see. I bent over, put my face right on the surface. The splashes continued. The trout were eating something that wasn't there. I took off my hat and held it in the current. Against the band appeared tiny grey worms with the stubs of half-formed wings. Nothing that Gramp had tied was anything like them.

I looked back at the trees. Had he truly been there, I wouldn't have been surprised, for I felt closer to him at that moment than ever I had before. There was a dimension to flyfishing I had never imagined. That morning, as long as they allowed, I sat watching trout feed on invisible bugs.

The next day I went with my mother on her weekly trip into town to buy groceries and asked her to drop me at the library. She couldn't have been happier, of course, thinking that I had finally gotten serious about school, but the books I was looking for were books about fly fishing and fly tying, and I found one about entomology and put it conspicuously atop the stack I checked out. Mom pronounced the word silently in the car later and smiled and nodded her head.

I read everything I could get my hands on. Any spare money I came by was spent on fishing books. I collected bug samples from the stream and peered at them through a magnifying glass. I began to tie new patterns, some of them more powerful as trout catchers than the ones Gramp had showed me. I learned about egg laying and emergence and spinner falls, water temperature and behaviorial drift. All this impressed Jerry, and sometimes, when he'd find the time to come along, I'd outfish him. He'd say, "What the hell are you using?" I'd hand him one of my imitations, tell him how to fish it. "What is it?" he'd say. "It's just a fly," I'd say. "I've never seen one like this, where'd you get the idea for it?" I shrugged my shoulders. "Well, what do you call it?" "Pale Morning Dun," I'd say, and turn so he couldn't see my smile.

But most of the time I was alone. I spent a lot of time sitting on the bank watching the water. That was as important to me now as fishing itself. In all this I felt closer and closer to Gramp, who, it sometimes seemed, was in the trees behind me, watching and smiling. I usually went upstream, though, and did not like going down, unless I had to, and then only as far as the pool above Horseman's Run. I could not bring myself to fish Horseman's Run alone.

The meaning of it all, to a mind as young as my own, was a respect for trout I had never found when it mattered how many I caught. Knowing them, their behavior, habits and needs, made it impossible for me to intentionally harm them. It even seemed unfair to create a pattern that would more easily trick them. Their beauty, bravery and innocence humbled me. Gramp was right. They were too noble to kill. I had to release every one I caught.

The time came finally to leave. The nearest college was fifty miles away, but I wanted to go to the University with Jerry, and that was another hundred, and there were no streams. It was as though that part of my life went on hold while I studied for what I thought then was more important. Alison was there and it wasn't long before I had a girl. Everything was serious. Everything mattered.

I had never really experienced anything like what I found away from home. The University was old and right in the middle of the city, and they had a brick wall around it. The stuff I'd seen only on television roamed the streets outside. Gangs, drive-by shootings, car-jackings, armed robberies. The first week I was there a girl who lived in the dormitory with Alison was raped. A lot of the city people had moved to the suburbs, but apparently that wasn't far enough because, with regularity, somebody got mugged or held up out there where the lawn grew.

I knew even then that it was a matter of time before our small part of the world was discovered by refugees. A few homes had been built before Gramp died. People had moved in from towns as small as Leavitt and Gardiner. What would happen when the suburbs themselves let loose? People wanted land and trees and no burglar alarms or bars on the windows. Who could blame them for envying the safety and beauty I had always known? Though life in the city rewarded initiative, and Jerry found the excitement of being there almost as stimulating as Alison, I was of a different mind. I decided that, when my education was done, I would return home. I knew that what was along the stream where my grandfather had taught me to fish was more important than anything else the world could offer, and, though I might not become as prosperous or as famous as Jerry, who had decided to be a big-time trial lawyer, I would make my way, and I would have the stream.

I managed to get home sometimes, on holidays usually, and I always felt guilty when it was time to go. I couldn't fish in the off-season, and I stayed at school to help earn money during the summer. Jerry often wasn't with me anyway, and, worst of all, Gram was slowing down. She sat a lot looking out the window at the hill where Gramp had watched the sunset. She was hard of hearing and did not like asking you to repeat what you said, so she had started talking to herself, always about the past. She didn't talk really, she whispered, just loud enough so you could hear if you were close. Maybe that was because she was hard of hearing to herself as well, I don't know, but I thought of Gramp a lot when I was with her now, stooped and busy with her loneliness.

And then she died.

It was the end of my junior year in the spring, with Jerry one term ahead and almost done with pre-law. We went home. Neither of us said much the whole 150 miles. I knew he was going over everything and how, with Gram dead, something had closed, and we would truly drift apart.

After the funeral we all sat around remembering. Mom got out the old pictures. I hadn't seen them since I was a kid and was struck again at how beautiful Gram had been and that Gramp was so tall, standing beside her.

"She was the most beautiful woman in the county," Mom said, tapping one of the pictures.

There was Gram in a long white dress and her hair on top of her head and on either side, two tall men dressed in suits with high collars. I recognized Gramp. He was thinner, with a long chin.

"Who's the other guy?" I asked.

"Mr. Fario," Mom said.

Jerry and I looked at each other. We stared at the photograph of three people, two of whom were so close and had shared our lives so fully, and this other, who had lurked always around the edges. Mom took the picture of Gram and Gramp and Mr. Fario out of the album and set it on the table.

"He was a fisherman too," she said, "but with bait. He never threw anything back. Finally Gramp would have none of it." She tapped the photo. "I always thought that was so sad." She shook her head. "The place has been sold, you know. A doctor and his wife from Livingston bought it. Want the peace and quiet of the country, I suppose. This whole area will be filled some day, you just watch."

Jerry and I drove out to the old house. Nothing was there, only the frame, floor and roofbeams and the shell of the portico, which hung now over steps that were full of light. The half dead trees were gone. The ground had been plowed and graded. Everything had been cleared from the back. Two men were unloading fresh lumber from a big truck and stacking it to one side. We walked over.

"Well, I guess they saved the shell," I said to one of the men, "but that's not much. We're neighbors."

He shook his head. "It's going too. The interior wood was okay. That's why we took it down piece by piece, and those beams. The old stuff looks good as trim, but it's going right to the ground. They're starting over."

"From the ground up?" I asked.

"Everything," the man said.

We went to the cellar. The door was gone. The heavy concrete steps dropped away, and even now, with the house virtually demolished, the sunlight like a clean, new wave everywhere, at the bottom of the steps was a darkness as profound as night.

"Let's take a look," Jerry said. He put a foot on the first step. I didn't move. "What's the matter?" Jerry said.

I shrugged.

"That's what we always wanted to do, get a peek down there."

"I know."

"Well, c'mon, then."

"Jerry, let's go fishing."

"Fishing."

"We haven't gone fishing for a long time."

"You don't want to go down there."

"It's just a hole."

We stood, Jerry with one foot in and me floating helplessly. Then he said, "Screw it, maybe there's a hatch," and we left.

A letter came at school ten days later, only it wasn't a letter, just an envelope with Mom's handwriting. Inside was a clipping from the Livingston Herald. The cellar had been torn up. Beneath layers of concrete they had found the remains of three young boys, neatly in a row. They took Fario out of the cemetery and put him into the ground behind the state penitentiary in Jefferson County.

I did not go home for a long while after that, and I never spoke to Mother about the sons who had been spared in childhood. She never said a word to me.

I went to the river. The water beneath the big oak was gloomy and still, but I knew that, momentarily, light would come and, one by one, miniature sails would appear. To have a chance at life, each pale dun for a time must drift, ignorant of the forms that wait below. That seems to me now eminently fair, and when I too can no longer see the fly, where else would you expect me to be but here, on Horseman's Run, waiting for a rise.

Match The Hatch

I walked away from Point of Rocks toward the spot where the creek makes that big turn toward the Conservancy. Jay was in his camper, but Greg was out of his fifth wheel leaning against the wooden fence smoking. A trout rose against the far bank.

It was the start of the season on Silver Creek in Idaho. I was here for the brown drake hatch. Anyone who fishes the hatch knows that it is a crap shoot. But when the drakes are up, big trout hold in the channels feeding, all the big trout in Silver Creek.

I reached the bend of the creek, keeping to the left trail and not the right, which leads to the willows further upstream. Fishing the willows is fine, but a wooden plank rests at the water line at the bend, and I love sitting there with my boots in the water on the first day. I am lately not much for the Conservancy, which has a fly shop quality. The Conservancy is in the magazines. Pictures are in the tiny hut at the top of the Conservancy, and someone is there to explain about Silver Creek, so that you become humble, along with everyone else who signs the little book outside.

I like it where the guides don't go. I sit on the wooden plank with my boots in the water. I imagine that everything is the same.

I looked at the water, green and oily smooth above the weed beds. I didn't think about trout particularly or about beauty or even that, perhaps, it was not the same. I thought about Jay, who came from Maine, and Greg, who came from Portland, and me, from California. We were Silver Creek afi-cionados. We were here for the brown drake hatch. We didn't know each other, truly, but we were on Silver Creek at the opening of the trout season, hoping for brown drakes. We were brown drake brothers.

Sometimes I e-mail Greg, or he e-mails me. I am on Greg's generic list for e-mails. He sends regular bulletins about the doctors and how his legs are doing. These are informational Greg bulletins. I'm not singled out. But we are fly tiers, so we exchange patterns, and then he tells me where he is specifically and specifically what he is doing. In the fall and winter he hits casinos in New Jersey and Florida. He parks the fifth wheel in the casino lot. He plays poker. He's pretty good at it. This past winter he won his first poker tournament. Greg is divorced too and travels around living in that fifth wheel. In the summer he fishes all over the Rockies. Greg is a trout bum. He lives the life of a trout bum, but he can't hike the streams now. He is an ex-lawyer with bad legs. It's hereditary. There's a name for it. It's eating him alive. So he lives like a trout bum until he can't live anymore. He'll die like a trout bum, slumped across his float tube, somewhere on a lake or river, maybe Silver Creek, maybe during the brown drake hatch, but, hopefully, not until the hatch is done. I don't want to come across Greg floating, face down, through a pod of rising trout.

Greg is one helluva cook. He stuffs Cornish game hens. He creates pastry you wouldn't find in any bakery, not even in San Francisco. Greg says he never lost a case, but he can't stand now for any length of time. He can't stand for the defense. He is on permanent disability, without wife or kids, a custom fly-tying bench in the nose of his fifth wheel. He floats in a tube. He pleads his case before brown trout and rainbows. He hopes that the jury stays out until the hatch is over.

I don't know much about Jay. He was a commercial fisherman. Something happened at sea. Greg says Jay still lives in Maine because his kids live there. Jay drives the camper to Silver Creek. Greg meets him sometimes at the San Juan River in New Mexico, sometimes on the Thompson in Montana. I've not seen Jay fish anyplace on Silver Creek except where he parks the camper at Point of Rocks. Greg says it's something about the accident and the current of a river and his spine. Jay uses a wading staff. No one uses a wading staff on Silver Creek because the bottom is silty. But Jay uses a wading staff.

I sat a bit longer. A trout rose in the middle of the creek above the weed beds. The rise turned me away from thinking. But it was only that one rise. I leaned back on both hands. After awhile I stood. I walked upstream about three hundred yards, sat down on the bank and slid into the water.

The current swirled above my knees. The bottom was grassy and soft. I waded out to the middle and faced downstream.

I was using a five weight graphite rod, a furled leader and four feet of tippet. To the tippet I had knotted a size-18 barbless gold bead head with a spiky, moss-green body. I made a thirty-foot cast directly across to the bank and threw a downstream mend after it. I let the mend belly. Then, holding the rod tip low and directly in front of me, I jigged the bead head slowly away from the bank until it reached a position straight below. When the line straightened, I allowed the bead head to hang a moment. I lifted the rod a bit and dropped it back. I lifted the rod again and dropped it back. Then I took a few steps downriver, made a false cast and laid the bead head out near the bank and repeated the process. I fished that way, mending and jigging, the entire three hundred yards and picked up two nice rainbows about sixteen or seventeen inches in length. I say sixteen or seventeen because my net opening is seventeen inches, and the two rainbows were just shy of that, bowing in the soft mesh of the net. So I'll say sixteen inches, but maybe it was seventeen.

I was satisfied. I was fishing Silver Creek, the best spring creek west of the Mississippi. Hell, west of anywhere. This was Silver Creek, and I knew what to do.

I walked back to the parking area at Point of Rocks. Jay and Greg were in their waders, leaning against the wooden fence watching a fly fisherman. I saw from the license plate of the vehicle next to mine that he was from the Bay Area.

Everything about the guy was new. New waders. New shirt. New Tyrolean hat, a bright feather in the band. New net and fishing vest. He was out of an Orvis catalog. A cigar was crimped in the corner of his mouth. He stood in Jay's spot, where the bottom wasn't soft. Jay's waders were wet.

"How did you do?" Greg asked.

I wanted to fill my net. I wanted to say seventeen inches. If it had been anyone else, I probably would have said seventeen inches. Maybe even eighteen. The trout did bow the net.

"Two," I said. "Sixteen inches."

Greg smiled. We watched Bay Area fish Jay's spot. Bay Area's casting was terrible.

"What's going on?" I asked, pointing with my rod.

"He moved in," Greg said.

"He what?"

"He was up above, fishing down. He fished into Jay. It's pretty obvious he's a beginner."

"He's an asshole," I said.

"He doesn't know any better," Greg said. "Look at him."

"He needs to be educated," I said.

Jay shook his head. Jay was five-eight, maybe five-nine, thin, older than his years, older than Greg or I. It was hard to tell just how old Jay was, but he was frail, placed into his oversize waders, which had no belt but were held up loosely by broad, camouflaged suspenders. He looked like an old whaler on the deck of a wooden ship in one of those History Channel documentaries.

"Never mind," Jay said. "He'll be out in a while."

"Look at him," I laughed. "He's standing right where he should be fishing. Somebody should educate him."

Jay shook his head. "If he asks. Otherwise, never mind."

"That's your spot."

"My name's not on it," Jay said. "Forget it."

I looked at Jay. I looked at Bay Area. I hated amateurs.

"Well," Greg said. "What do you say to a couple sandwiches and a bottle of beer. I have an extra tube. Let's put in at the three pines and float down through the Purdy section to the Picabo bridge."

"Sure," I said. "Sounds good to me."

Jay couldn't make it. Jay had that spine.

"I have three steaks in the frig," Greg said. "We'll have steaks tonight, garlic mashed potatoes, carrots and peas and German chocolate cake I made for dessert. Then we'll wait for the drakes. They ought to pop near sunset."

"Are they up this far already?" I asked.

"I've seen some below," Greg said. "They're moving up-river."

"That great," I said. "I've got plenty of duns and spinners tied up."

"I have a new pattern or two myself. Like to see them?"

"You bet," I grinned. "I'll probably be borrowing a couple anyway. Your ties work better than mine." I liked flattering Greg.

Greg grinned. He liked being flattered. Maybe it was the lawyer that couldn't stand on his feet anymore. I was sorry about Greg. It was too bad he could not hike the streams and get back in where the Bay Areas wouldn't go. I was sorry that Jay could only fish where Silver Creek flowed gently in front of his camper. Bay Area continued to splash and foul Jay's spot. Jay removed his waders. He dropped them over the fence, climbed slowly up into the camper and closed the door.

Greg and I walked to the fifth-wheel. Greg cut thick slices of Italian salami from a roll, peeling the gray, marbly skin with the edge of the knife. He cut thick wedges of red onion and thick slices of white bakery bread. He smeared the bread with mayonnaise. As an afterthought he included a thick square of cheddar cheese. He closed the sandwiches.

"You only live once," he grinned.

We ate the sandwiches and drank the beer, ice cold from the chest he kept filled under the fold-down table. We talked about fly tying and the fly shops in Ketchum. We talked about school and other places we had fished and some about women and why they had left. But mostly we talked about Silver Creek and how grand it was when big trout came up for the brown drakes. Greg was all right. He was a lawyer, but an ex-lawyer. He never talked about law, except to say that he could not do it anymore.

"Along with everything else," he laughed.

We compared flies.

Then we put the tubes and tackle into the bed of his pickup. I followed in my Jeep to the three pines, where we dropped everything off. Then we took both vehicles down to the take-out, left the truck and drove in the Jeep back to the put-in. We picked up the rods, slung the inflated tubes over our backs, holding them by the strap, and walked through the opening in the barbed wire fence down to the creek. It was tough for Greg, but this was Silver Creek.

The water was clear and glassy smooth. We stepped into the tubes, pulled the tubes up to our waists, then sat on the weedy bank and slid into the water. We squatted onto the strap harness fastened underneath the tubes and were suspended, floating like gigantic corks on Silver Creek.

I let Greg go ahead. I wanted him to have the first shot. I did not want to feel sorry for Greg or Jay, but I did feel sorry. I had my legs and my back and my spine. I could fish anywhere anyway anytime. Something was eating Greg. He had doctors and medicine and Vicodin, but something was eating Greg.

The sun moved over in the blue, cloudless Idaho sky and was now at our backs. We floated, fishing languidly. I watched Greg. He was a good fisherman. There was as yet no hatch, so he fished a soft hackle, working it down ahead of him, planting his feet against the silty bottom now and again at a particularly good spot. I liked soft hackles. Besides Greg, I was the only guy I knew who fished soft hackles, which are as old as fly fishing is old. I was proud to know this and that Greg knew this and that we fished soft hackles together.

Greg was all right in that tube. He was as good as anybody else fishing. He was as good as I was. Bay Area, in his Tyrolean hat, his Orvis catalog, puffing a black cigar, did not know that he was a fool. He was no fly fisherman. He was a fool who was fly fishing.

We floated down to the Jeep. It took two hours. I got a couple more rainbows. Greg got three trout, one almost twenty inches, a deep-bellied brown that fell for a size eight soft hackle. The brown took Greg into his backing. We scrambled out of the harness. I handed Greg my rod and slung both tubes over my back, one in each hand. I felt professional climbing up to the truck. I moved slowly so I would not get ahead of Greg. We chattered about the impending hatch, about brown drake patterns and about how we hadn't seen anything yet, how the hatch would bring up all the old grandfathers in the creek and how we would fight them in the almost-dark. I was very happy and very professional.

We drove up to the Jeep. I followed Greg back to Point of Rocks. Bay Area was gone, but a few other vehicles had arrived, all with Idaho plates. Greg got the barbecue going. Jay came over with a bottle of cabernet. We sat around drinking wine out of water glasses and wondering about the brown drakes and if they would come off. It was good talking. Other fishermen sat around in their waders, talking and waiting. Some came over. It was all very good and very happy and very professional. Everyone was here for the drakes. Everyone knew what to do. Greg put on the steaks. Then we sat eating, drinking cabernet from our water glasses, talking about the hatch and all quite professional and happy, veterans of combat, eager for another battle.

Jay was relaxed. He talked about his sons, who lived in Maine, and his wife, who had died long ago. His sons had always wanted him to re-marry, but he had had enough of that, and now fly fishing was all there was. It was all he had ever truly wanted to do. It was all any of us had ever wanted, and though I did not talk about it, everything for me now was the same, except the fishing, which was the first time always and always with the same feeling. Nobody understands who is not a fly fisherman. I was very happy, sitting in the canvas chair, sipping red wine from a water glass, with Greg and Jay and the other fly fishermen, smoking, laughing and talking. The light fell. We waited for dimples to appear on the glass-smooth current of Silver Creek.

Then someone yelled, "There!"

We grabbed our rods and hurried to the stream. The light was a sheen wrinkling the dark surface. I saw a dimple, then another.

We took up stations twenty yards apart, strung out upriver, some ten or twelve of us. I did not like the crowd, but there was no other way, with this hatch. The drakes were coming just here, and the trout were here after them, so here we were.

Someone cried, "Fish on!" Someone else laughed.

I cast my parachute dun carefully three feet above a rise, just upriver of my position.

We fished that way for twenty minutes, hooking and releasing big trout. Headlights appeared in the parking area. The drakes had rung the dinner bell. Other fishermen were coming down for the feast.

I heard a splash upstream on the far side. A fisherman waded down, in a line where the trout were rising. It was Bay Area, in that dumb Tyrolean hat and Orvis catalog. He was hysterical. He waded right through where he should have been fishing.

Greg was just down from me. Jay was on the other side of Greg, standing in his spot.

Greg struggled with pain even to be standing there. Jay's legs were apart. He balanced like a tight rope walker, the wading staff trailing down current behind him, tethered to his vest.

"What the hell!" I called. "You bastard! Get out of there!"

"The trout," Bay Area blubbered. "Look at them. Look at the trout."

He came on like a madman.

Greg pushed away. He almost fell. Jay tried to swing around.

"You're fishing right through us!" I yelled.

"But the trout!" Bay Area said. "Look at the trout!"

I wanted to go out after him. I wanted to punch his goddamn face.

The drakes continued to pop, a regular flotilla of drakes, drifting like miniature, unmoored sailboats. Bay Area floundered toward Greg and Jay. His fly rod was a whip. His fly line slapped the water. All the trout went down.

"God damn you!" I yelled. I waded out a bit and popped him on the head with the tip of my rod. He was oblivious. He came on, spooking every trout around him.

"Don't," Greg called. He was almost to the bank, struggling painfully. "Let him be."

Bay Area was over Greg's position and heading for Jay's. Jay turned awkwardly. He lost his balance, stabbing with his wading staff. He floundered out of the creek.

Greg and Jay stood watching Bay Area move down into Jay's position, where he stopped, gaping at the water. The drakes, after hesitating, continued to blimp up. Bay Area was helpless.

I strode up to Greg and Jay. I said, "The sonofabitch. Right in your spot, Jay. He took your spot again. He screwed everything."

"Let him be," Jay said.

"He crowded us out!" I declared.

"It doesn't matter," Jay said. "You shouldn't have done that."

"But that's your spot," I said. "He crowded you out of your spot again."

"It doesn't matter," Jay said. "He doesn't know. There are other days. Mind your business."

Jay dropped his waders. He laid them over the rail of the fence. He leaned his rod against the fence, climbed into the camper and shut the door.

I looked at Greg. Greg shook his head. He limped toward the fifth wheel.

Bay Area stood dumbfounded among the brown drakes. The trout rose. I wanted to be in the water. I had come all this way. I wanted to fish the brown drake hatch.

My face grew hot. I looked at the camper. I looked at the fifth wheel. I cursed Bay Area. I cursed the unmoored sails drifting, almost invisibly now, upon Silver Creek. Then I cursed myself for being so stupid, so goddamn stupid.

Chasing The Whale

The embers of the fire glowed.

"Let's finish this off," Greg said.

I held out my glass. The gin and vermouth gleamed in the pitcher. The ice made a pleasant tap that reminded me of something I could not remember.

"Tell me," I said.

"His son Tom called from Maine."

"Where was Jay?"

"In New Mexico, on the San Juan. He had dinner outside with a couple friends after fishing."

Greg paused.

"What then?"

"He wanted to read before turning in for the night. I never knew anyone who read so much as Jay, and all classics. He wasn't out of the camper the next morning. They found him slumped over the table with a book in his hand."

A trout splashed beyond the lodge pole fence. The sun was behind the mountain. A last amber shine touched the stream. The ring came into the shine. The trout splashed again near the far bank.

Each June I drove to Silver Creek in Idaho for the brown drake hatch. Jay's camper was always parked there against the lodge pole fence. Greg's trailer was always cramped under the willows.

"Jay's dead," Greg finished.

We sat drinking. A prosthetic leg rested against Greg's camp stool. The stump of Greg's right knee protruded from the stool. The stump was wrapped in surgical tape to control the swelling while he floated in that patched red tube. Fishing from a tube was what Greg did now. That was fine, since Silver Creek was a bath tub all the way through the Double R Ranch, under the Highway 20 bridge and around through the grain fields to the Picabo Store, where it turned to oblivion in the high desert.

Greg was chasing the whale. He lived in that trailer. After the divorce and the disability from the law firm in Portland, he wanted no more of wives and houses. He wanted to go wherever, whenever. He was a trout bum, the only one-legged trout bum I ever knew. He kept a monthly journal. In the journal he saw birds, game, wild flowers. He saw the flies he tied, how he fished the flies, how many trout he caught, how big they were and where he caught them. He saw the people he met, what he prepared for dinner and how he managed everything on one, true leg and that other of titanium with an articulated foot.

Jay was a trout bum too. We talked sometimes in Greg's trailer, while Greg unstrapped the leg or made the coffee. Greg was not bitter. Sometimes he laughed about the leg and called himself Ahab in a tube. We laughed too. Jay named the tube Pequod.

Greg loved to cook. Some evenings Jay and I sat in Greg's trailer bullshitting while Greg prepared dinner, pushing about the tiny kitchen floor in the swivel chair he used for fly tying. Jay talked about life in the navy and then in the merchant marine. He talked about running a small lobster boat, hauling traps alone, often in the dark, until he broke his back in a storm and could no longer go to sea. He could still fish, however, if he remained in one spot. He fished for Atlantic salmon in the rivers around home. After two wives and two grown sons, he discovered trout fishing and roamed the Rockies chasing the whale. He and Greg had met years before here at Silver Creek.

They traveled together sometimes, at a pace set by seasons, streams and hatches. I was not a bum. I was held by an acre and a half of land in the San Joaquin Valley of California, with two weeks here, two weeks there, returned always by appointments, held mail or roof repair. I was a hitchhiker, thumb up, looking, from time to time, for a ride upon the open stream.

"He lived the way he wanted to live," Greg finished.

"That's what counts" I said.

I looked at Greg's titanium leg. He had an additional leg fitted permanently into his waders so he could more easily step in or out. He had back-up legs hanging like trophies over the bay window of the trailer. He no longer walked or waded. He sat in the red float tube, anywhere the water was flat, here or on the Henry's Fork or the Jefferson and Missouri in Montana or the San Juan in New Mexico. He had diabetes. He ate a rainbow of pills.

I knew Greg and Jay only from the first two weeks of each June at Silver Creek, when the drakes are up and every big trout feeds voraciously.

"You want to float the Double R tomorrow?" he said.

"Yes," I replied. Only members of a private club fished the Double R, and members could take a guest.

"Around nine, then," Greg said. "You can use my spare tube."

"All right," I said.

The following morning was soft and sunlit. There was no wind. I put my gear into the bed of Greg's truck. Greg had the gas pedal moved over under the left foot.

We arrived at the ranch, parked along the stream and put on the waders. I watched Greg with admiration and guilt.

Finally he pulled the tube up around his waist and slid heavily into the stream. I sat down beside him. We pushed off.

The water was soundlessly smooth. The small, universal things appeared and drifted by. I felt the peace I felt no where else.

Greg was ahead. I watched his rod lift back and forward, the line turning forward in a narrow sinew of strength, the rhythm of all true fly fishermen and the comrade who comes when practice becomes art. Jay was the best fly fisherman I ever saw. Greg was close. But the lobsterman from Maine, who died reading the classics, was a ballet with a fly rod.

For a time, however, it had not mattered. I wanted Greg to catch trout. I wanted him to catch big trout, so many big trout that he might believe, as I did, that there is relief in chasing the whale. I had had my own operation months before, the kind of operation that makes one think about selling everything and maybe buying a fifth wheel or a camper or a trailer and be a vagrant of the sun. There is always pursuit. Even if there is no capture, pursuit is good enough.

That evening we sat outside Greg's trailer before a bed of coals sipping drinks and listening to trout hunting in the shallows. Greg had prepared his grandmother's chicken casserole. He had baked a chocolate cake. We sat outside eating, talking and drinking the drinks Greg poured from the pitcher.

"Tell me the rest of it," I said.

Greg watched me above the coals.

"Tom and his brother flew down to the San Juan from Maine. Jay was in one of those parlors. They cremated him. They put him in a brass urn. Then they put the urn in the camper and drove back to Maine."

"It's good that Jay got home," I said.

"He's not home," Greg said.

I tried to see Greg's eyes.

144

"What do you mean?" I asked.

"Jay had an old canoe. Some Indians gave it to him when he was a kid. He used the canoe to fish for Atlantic salmon in the river where he lived."

Greg hesitated. The embers were dark. I couldn't see Greg's eyes.

"At dawn Tom and and his brother put the urn in the canoe. They set the canoe on fire and pushed it out into the river."

I had nothing to say. I saw Jay. I saw the burning canoe, drifting to the open sea. I saw a rising sun, whose dying flame one day would devour the world.

The Trophy Of A Life Time

My brother Frank died of a heart attack twelve years ago on a five-day float down the Sutton River in Northern Ontario. We were fly fishing for large Brook trout. It was three days into the float in the middle of nowhere. The plane would not retrieve us for two more days. The guide, a scruffy, muscular, sallow-faced man named Charlie, put Frank in the stern of the canoe under a green canvas. I told Charlie to paddle like hell. Charlie said, wasn't Frank dead, and wouldn't he be dead all along the river, no matter where we waited, so why not keep fishing, wasn't that why we were there? What was the difference in waiting, Charlie said, on the river and fishing or waiting at the pick up and just waiting? Two days were two days we had paid for. So I sat in the bow of the canoe hooking one Brook trout after another, my dead brother in the stern of the canoe under a green canvas. That night, awake, I thought of Frank under the canvas, and the next day I fished again. Frank was under the canvas until the float plane came to take us out.

I have four hundred books in my fly fishing library, books on how to catch trout, where to catch trout in stream, river or still water, books on the best places anywhere, the remote places in New Zealand, Patagonia, Alaska, Canada, Russia, the chalk streams of Great Britain, anywhere that trout may be bigger than any trout before. I lost two jobs and a wife to fly fishing. I have no house. I mow no lawn. I keep no dog or cat. I have two dozen of the best fly rods money can buy—Sage, Orvis, Winston, Loomis. I have a score of reels, none under three hundred dollars, with extra spools and fly lines—Lamson, Ross, Hardy. I buy the latest equipment—vests, boots, wading staffs. I order a new set of waders each year—Simms, top of the line. I tie flies. I buy Japanese hooks. I'm on the mailing lists for materials from a dozen suppliers around the world. In addition, I have hundreds of tapes—how to stalk trout, how to read trout water, how to tie the best Blue Wing Olives, Pale Morning Duns; how to create nymphs, emergers, crippled duns, spinners. I tie secret, trout-devastating flies. I want The Big One. The Biggest One. I'm the Ahab of trout fishing.

Frank has been gone twelve years. He's in the stern of a canoe under a green canvas. I take Frank to every riffle, run or pool. I carry Frank like a sack of ashes. There is no loneliness more lonely than to be on a trout stream with a dead brother I never truly knew. Around that bend, behind that hill, under that fading sun, he appears, a shadow Frank from the shadow-world of childhood. We were not strangers while fly fishing, not aliens, cast into life in the seed of a father who betrayed everything a father was never to betray. I only knew my brother, fly fishing on silver waters.

There have been many places since, many adventures. I keep no log. I have no records. I carry no camera. Memories are previews on a movie screen. My brain is filled by gone attractions. Frank had a camera. He was a fanatic about a camera. He wanted to keep something. He took pictures of every trip. His camera was under the green canvas. I don't know where the pictures are. I don't care about any pictures. His ex-wife went through everything. She wanted to know, would I want a photo from here or a photo from there? There were photos our father took when we were kids fishing the Mokelumne River in the Sierras. Frank was the guardian of all photos. What would I want with photos? No, I said. Photographs are headstones in the cemetery of fly fishing. There are no cameras after life. Things are where they are.

Apart from private time—vacations, holidays—I have been fortunate in work that allows me to travel. I don't take planes, unless absolutely necessary-the Hildreth Project is an example of that. I don't ride trains. I drive a Ford 150 cab-over, top of the line, four-wheel drive. I leave early, always with a five-weight Sage and a three-weight Orvis. I pack my Simms waders, my Simms vest and boots and an assortment of flies in special aluminum boxes I had made for the purpose. I keep a sub-nosed 38 under the seat. In this day and age, who knows what's fishing around the next bend?

I eat chicken fried steak with sausage gravy and mashed potatoes in dumpy little towns along the way. I seek out back roads for places unheard of, places off logging roads or on topographical maps. I have found many places to check out on an afternoon or on a morning before I move on to some other diner that serves chicken fried steak with sausage gravy and mashed potatoes. I have no loyalties. The people I meet I don't remember after the next people I meet. Things are where they are.

I have discarded everything. I am not bound by fishing pals, who want always to return to familiar places, with campsites, stone fire-pits and rusted barbecue grills they've used again and again. No place holds charm once it has been fished. I have no pieties. Days are evanescent. I try every new tippet material, every new tying material, every new book or dvd. I want The One. The Big One. The Trophy of a Lifetime. I want Him on a five-weight rod, a #16 Pale Morning Dun and 6X tippet. In the name of an unknowable brother, lost in the wilderness of Northern Ontario, I want The Whale.

I stop at every fly shop along the way. One day in North Eastern Idaho, in a tiny shop, stuck back in the corner of a hardware store, a man told me of a small stream outside of town that hardly anyone fished, not even the locals. The pools were few and far between, the runs and riffles covered by thin veils of water. He told me about a pool under an abandoned wooden bridge. I had nowhere to be until the following afternoon. "You'll have to walk," the man said, and gave me directions.

The road went up through stands of pines that had been logged long ago. New pines had been planted. I went back in about five miles. The road flattened, then dropped and turned down to a shining ribbon of water. I don't know if the creek had a name. I named it Nowhere Creek. I stopped the truck at the nearest point, before the road turned away and disappeared among the pines. A dirty, fender-bent Jeep was parked there, the kind used in The Second War. Fly fisher's dread came over me. Someone had beaten me to it.

I put on my gear and started down. At the last rise before the final twenty yards to the stream, I stopped. Beneath a broken wooden bridge, a pipe stuck into his mouth, an old man was fishing.

I had a good angle down to the water. I saw dark shadows holding at the bottom of the pool. I saw the swirls of sand as the shadows turned, wavering, nosing into the current. An immense shadow hovered to one side.

The old man raised the rod and, with a deft turn of the wrist, set the fly down several feet upstream of where the pod of shadows lay. The fly drifted. A shadow rose. I felt my heels in the gravely dirt. I felt my rod hand tighten. That should be my hook in the corner of the mouth, my trout running for the far side of the pool, where a cottonwood tree, broken in a spring flood, had lodged up against the far bank, its dead branches jammed into the water.

The trout and the fly achieved a single point. The old man moved his shoulders, ever so slightly. The water boiled under the fly. The old man was stone. The fly drifted. A dark shape chased itself to the bottom of the pool.

The old man straightened. He puffed on his pipe. He took three steps upriver. Again, the deft flick of the wrist. Again, the fly, leader and line rolling out in a perfect loop, the line turning and the fly turning, parallel to the water, at the end of the tippet, falling like a dry blossom to the flat surface of the pool.

A second shadow rose. That point again. The bulge again and the swirling splash. The old man was a statue. The fly moved by. The shadow descended. Twice, and the old man had not raised the rod.

I stumbled down the embankment. "Excuse me," I said. "What are you doing?"

"Oh, hello," the old man said.

He was older than old. He wore a frayed baseball cap. Universal Trucking was stitched above the bill. He wore a faded plaid shirt that looked as though it had been turned inside out, faded jeans and a pair of hip boots that had been patched again and again with those patches boys use to repair the inner tubes of balloon tires. His vest was filthy. One of the pockets was torn away. He looked like a yellowed advertisement from an old Sears catalog. His fly rod was a cheap fiber glass Shakespeare. I hadn't seen a Shakespeare fiber glass in years. I hadn't seen his reel on any stream. It was an old black Pflueger, dented around the rim, like an aluminum cup. His leader was monofilament, the kind my father used to soften between the moistened felt pads of a leader book.

"Why don't you strike?" I asked.

"I don't want to strike," he said.

"Not strike? How can you catch anything if you don't set the hook?"

"I don't have a hook," he said.

"No hook?"

The old man smiled, relit his pipe and looked off across the stream to the far bank, which rose to meet a stand of cottonwood trees, whose powdery fluff lifted and spun on the summer air. He held the line between the thumb and first finger of his rod hand. With his other hand he drew the line back. At the end of the tippet was a small gob of feathers and fur that looked as though it had been swept from a carpet and mixed in a blender. The hook was snipped at the bend.

"What are you doing?" I asked, shaking my head. "You can't catch anything that way."

"I catch all my trout this way now," he said.

"That doesn't make sense," I grinned. "No hook. No trout. You might as well fish in your bathtub."

"I catch what I want to catch," the old man smiled.

"You're fooling me."

The old man put his eyes on my face. "My name is Ronald," he said.

"Wilson," I said.

"Well, Wilson," he said, "I've fished a long life. I've caught a lot of trout. I catch them in my sleep." He puffed on the pipe. "This fishing for trout," he said. "It's over—and—over, wouldn't you say?"

"Not when you're fishing for the big one."

"Well, now, that's just what I mean," he said.

"The trophy of a lifetime," I said. "That's what I'm after."

"My exact thought," he said.

"Then I don't get it," I said. "What are you doing?"

The old man tapped his head with the stem of his pipe. "Fly fishing, Wilson," he said. "I'm after the trophy of a lifetime."

I laughed. "Now you've really lost me. I've never seen anyone fish not to catch fish."

"I was that way myself for a long time. Look. On a quiet, deep pool like this, you can see right down to the bottom. So maybe, let's say, here comes one. You're like a spring, a tightening spring. In your hands. In your neck and shoulders. On your tongue. Wait now. Wait a bit more. Wait until he opens that mouth and turns down. You've done it so many times. You've done it in your sleep. The feeling, Wilson. How can you get ever used to a feeling you can never get used to? Gently with the rod. He'll hook himself, if you let him. Now, Wilson, let the line go when he goes. Gather the line when he comes. Like a violin, Wilson. Play him. Move the rod. Side to side with the rod. He'll tire himself. Bring him gently when he's tired. Ever more gently when he's truly tired. It's taken a lifetime to learn how to let him be tired. Easy with that net. You can lose him with the net. Now, there, in the net, he's yours! Look around, Wilson. No one to tell the story? Why not mount him? He's forever yours on a wall." The old man's body was dancing. "But I don't set the hook."

I held my breath. He was a marvelous, weird old man.

"Well, all right. Well and good, I suppose. But, why? Duck hunters don't go duck hunting not to shoot ducks."

"The biggest one we can catch. The record. That's what we're after."

"That's what I'm after."

I looked down at the immense shadow holding, just off from the other shadows, in a swirl of sand and current at the bottom of the pool. My mouth was dry looking at him.

"Wilson," the old man said, "when I was a boy, my mother took me to the department store when she went shopping. It was a big store—at least it seemed that way at the time. It was called Weber's Department Store, and took up most of the block. My mother gave me fifty cents for an ice cream soda and left me at the fountain. They had a candy counter there.

I drank my soda and stood in front of the counter. I stared at the candy. They had Bordeaux chocolate, chocolate truffles, chocolate peanut clusters. They had chocolate cherry cordials, chocolate caramel chews and chocolate molasses chips. When my mother returned from shopping, she bought me a piece of chocolate for being so patient." The old man laughed. "I learned about patience standing in front of a candy counter. When I go to any store now for any reason—if they have candy—I buy a Milky Way or a Hersheys or a Snickers. I can't help myself, Wilson. I love a Mounds Bar or a Three Musketeers or a Clark Bar. I can't resist chocolate. I've been trying to look at chocolate all my life and not eat chocolate. Chocolate is not good for me. I'm diabetic. But I love chocolate." He grinned. "Do you like chocolate, Wilson?"

"I love chocolate."

He pointed at the bottom of the pool.

"Look at them there," he said. "How beautiful. How fine they are. How can we not want to have them, Wilson, if only for a moment. But to have them, we must capture them. It's their power over us. Chocolate bars with fins."

"Fly fishing for chocolate," I laughed. "I've never heard that one before. I like it."

He pointed. "Chocolate bars, Wilson, lined up on a counter, wrapped in pretty liquid paper. That's their trick. That's how they hook us. We don't catch them. They get away. They're always waiting to hook us again. If you're a fly fisherman, isn't every trout in the stream the trophy of a lifetime?"

I wanted to see the old man's eyes. He was staring into the pool. I stared too. I thought, how many pools all over the world have I looked into just like this pool and seen trout just like these trout and wanted to catch every damned one of them. He had a point. There was a certain futility to fly fishing, a cer-tain over-and-over-and-get-nowhere. But that was true of anything. We eat. And when we're satisfied, do we throw away our refrigerators? Do we burn our recipes?

"One day," the old man said, "I wondered, what if maybe I fooled the trout before he fooled me. Maybe just watch him rise, take the fly, but do nothing. No reaction. No lifting the rod. No setting the hook. The trout just swims away. Now, I couldn't do that properly if the hook had a point. If he inhaled the fly and turned down, he might well hook himself, even if I lowered the rod. Besides, I didn't know that I could not set the hook. Automatic, right? Stimulus. Response. So I snipped the hook at the bend. The only thing then was, could I control myself when he rose to take the fly? Could I not react. Stimulus. But no response. Look here, Wilson."

I faced him. He waved his hand, stopping inches from my nose. I flinched and turned away.

"You see?" he said. "How could I not react after a lifetime of reacting? That's what I wanted to know. I have never been able to walk into any store that has chocolate and not buy chocolate."

"All right," I said. "An interesting exercise. I'll give you that. But, why? I've been to a lot of places for the biggest trout I could find. You're telling me I should go all the way down to Chile to fish the Rio Simpson, spend all that money and all that time and not have something to show for it? What am I proving? That's not any kind of fishing that I can see. That's some kind of mental game. I want the actual big one, right here in this net."

"I want him too, Wilson."

"Not without a hook." I grinned.

"Exactly without a hook. The only way is without a hook."

"But you said you didn't want to catch anything."

He tapped his head with the stem of the pipe. "The trophy of a lifetime."

I laughed. "Catch yourself? You're out of season."

He laughed too. "Walking into a candy store," he said, "and not buying chocolate because everything in me wants to buy chocolate."

He reached into his fly vest for a plastic, rectangular box that looked as though it had once held nails and screws. He removed a fly just like the one he had tied to his tippet. The fly had a hook point.

"Now you'll hook him," I declared.

"Yes, I suppose I might just hook him. But maybe that's the final thing. I'll cut the leader then. I want to know if I can not react when I know that I will hook him if I do. Not control anything, you see, by snipping the hook. Look here, Wilson. Would an alcoholic keep a bottle of bourbon around the house just to see if he could not take a drink?"

"Alcoholics can't do that," I said.

"I told myself that about my wife Margaret, six months ago, just before she died. We were married sixty years, Wilson. Sixty fine years. Could I keep something so dear and yet lose it? Could I live when someone I had lived with so long was no longer living with me? Inevitability, Wilson. I hate inevitability." He clenched a fist. "So I take a drink. So I eat a Snickers or a Milky Way I've hidden from myself, but know exactly where I've hidden it."

I stared at him. I didn't know what to say. I thought of Frank, alone under the green canvas.

"So, that's what I'm thinking now, Wilson. Put the glass to my lips and not drink. Put the chocolate bar into my mouth and not bite down. Leave the point on the hook and not strike. Visit Margaret's grave every day, each day, there in the park, under the shadow of a great oak, and want to live. That's what I have to catch."

"I'm so sorry," I said.

He smiled. "Wilson" he said, "when you're an old, old fly fisherman, like me, when the woman you've been with for sixty years is nowhere to be found, when you have only whiskey and chocolate bars and you're a diabetic, what do you do with loneliness? So I asked myself, can I start again? Can anything be saved? Chocolate, Wilson. Chocolate. Can a man love chocolate and learn to live without it?" He winked. "Now," he pointed, "there's another good pool a hundred yards upriver, around that next bend. Would it be too much for me to ask you to go on up there and just let me fish here alone?"

"A witness," I said. "Wouldn't you want a witness?"

"You'd like to know how I do?"

"I would," I said.

"Give me your address."

I gave him my address. We shook hands. He was a strange, interesting, perverse old man. I moved upstream and found the pool. It was a good pool. I did not catch anything to speak of. I fished for a frustating hour and walked back to the bridge. The old man was gone.

I finished the trip and headed home. On the road I thought about the old man. He was an odd, funny old man. He was the only fly fisherman I've met that I wouldn't mind talking to again. I never heard from him. After awhile I didn't think about him. I continued hunting The Whale.

One day, three years later, a UPS truck stopped at the tiny duplex I rented on 25th Street. The driver came out of the truck carrying an oddly shaped box. Inside the box was the glass rod, the Pflueger reel, the vest with one pocket torn away, the patched waders, the faded baseball cap that read Universal Trucking, the box of flies that looked as though they had been made from floor sweepings, and a felt wallet for moistening monofilament leaders.

I put the rod together. I attached the reel and strung the line, which was badly checked. I set the rod, reel, vest, cap, box of flies, waders and leader wallet in one corner of the small room. I picked up the package to throw away and found that I had missed a thin, white envelope. Inside the envelope was a note, which read, "Dear Wilson. I am Ronald's daughter. Father has passed away. He remembered you when he could no longer fish. He wanted you to have these things. He said that you were the one fly fisherman he truly enjoyed talking to, and that you would understand. Cordially, Evelyn.

I sat down in the cushioned chair. I looked at the old man's things. "I'll be damned," I said.

Big Two-Hearted River:
Part III

"There were plenty of days coming when he could fish the swamp."

When we were boys, the stream was not crowded. My brother and I walked the stream with our father. We watched him cast. We watched him work the tandem rig of flies across the white riffles. We watched him catch trout. We watched him put the trout into the wicker basket he carried under his arm, sprinkling the trout with wet grass and sweet fern. We carried wicker baskets. Sometimes we dipped the baskets into the stream to keep the trout cool and fresh. We sat by the water's edge. We watched our father clean the trout, slitting them from the vent hole up through the center of the jaw, taking everything out with one pull. He threw the guts onto the bank for the animals and birds. He washed the trout, swishing them back and forth in the current, pushing the stubborn, blood-black grit along the spine free with his thumb. We went back to camp. Our father fried the trout with the heads on for dinner. In the morning he used the grease for pancakes. The pancakes were crisp and shiny at the edges. Deer came down to drink or to cross the stream. There were bears.

One day, when we were still boys, our father no longer hiked the stream. He was fat. He smoked a pack a day. He drank. So he fished from a pram in the pond above the stream. My brother fished with him, for reasons that are complicated and have to do with our mother. I fished alone.

Our father died forty years ago and recently our mother died. My brother has been divorced. I have been divorced. We go to Chile to catch trout. We go to New Zealand and Alaska. We go to the trout streams of the Rockies. If he fishes up, I fish down. If he fishes down, I fish up. If we fish the same way, one of us goes on around and fishes ahead out of sight. Alone, I squint into the sun, waiting for a rise.

We no longer carry baskets. It is one of our few shared moralities. As the years passed, and the magazines appeared—all with the same cover—and the movie A River Runs Through It, the stream became crowded. Adorned by equipment worth thousands, scores of people were guided by men who wanted $500 to say, use this fly, stand over here, cast over there; who provided deli sandwiches with the crusts removed, pink champagne, quiche, tossed green salad, brownies made by the guide's wife or mother, and cloth napkins. The deer hide. The bears are in Canada.

My brother and I fish now mostly in Montana on a freestone river that comes out of the mountains and empties into the Yellowstone below Livingston. The land along the river, from the mouth to the state preserve, is privately owned. We know the ranchers. We fish in solitude. My brother fishes up. Or I fish up. He goes around. Or I go around.

I squint alone into the hot Montana sun.

I tie my own flies. Something is fine about hooking a trout with a fly you have made, fighting the trout until it wins or you win, and if you win, releasing the trout into the river, to watch it—blue and pink and silver—sink to a dark lair behind a stone that has been there thousands of years.

My brother is old now. I am older. We fish from morning until one or two. We go to the motel, have a drink, smoke a cigar, take a nap or walk around town. It's a small town. We know the people. They are friendly people. After the divorces we began coming here. We stay in the room together for two weeks, just the way we stayed together when we were boys. We don't talk about politics or religion. We don't talk about his kids or my kids. We talk about trout, how many, how big, how hard they fought, how many were lost that were bigger than any we caught. We talk about the people who own the ranches or live in the town.

When we first came here, everybody we knew was alive the following year. Ten years ago Harold Bromely died, then his wife Emma, who rode a wheelchair. A tort lawyer from Chicago bought Harold's ranch. The lawyer posted no trespassing signs along the river. He said it was his personal piece of paradise. He wants to buy Gordon Harber's ranch just above. Mae, Gordon's wife, died a few years back. We visited Mae in the nursing home. Orville Henderson, who was once a state senator, died at his ranch on the West Boulder. And Gordon Heath(there are two Gordons), who owns the dry goods store, just lost his wife. We ate dinner with Harold and Emma at the Country Pride and with Gordon and Mae at Prospector Pizza. Orville played the banjo for us the year he died. Gordon Heath was in the Navy in the Second World War and had a cruiser blown out from under him. We buy Gordon coffee at the drug store while we sip the best malteds this side of the Missouri River. I subscribe to The Pioneer, the town weekly, so I can have the people with me in California. I read the obituaries.

When I am on the stream, ahead of my brother or he ahead of me—having whistled and gone around—I think these things. I miss strikes.

My brother's knee goes out. He limps and wears a brace. Like a scarecrow, he stands in one place. Last year there was something about his stomach. He spent a night in a bathtub of warm water for relief, turning the hot water handle with his toes. The doctor talked about stomach lining and weak pockets. Old age, the doctor said. Drink fluids. Eat yogurt. I had an operation and take pills.

It's hard now sometimes for me to sleep. I try to fish my way there, but remembering the places and the trout keeps me interested, and I stay awake. My brother snores on the other bed. I fish in darkness. The water is above my waist. I can't see the fly. I can't see the rise. Something Cretaceous lifts the stream.

I met a fisherman. He was a lawyer too, but from Portland. I met him at Point of Rocks access to Silver Creek, east of Ketchum, Idaho. He had a red pickup and a fifth wheel. He parked at the access during the brown drake hatch, which comes off around Memorial Weekend and lasts eight or ten days. I chase the hatch too. I did not talk to him. He sat smiling alone sometimes in a canvas chair out front of the trailer. I was all the way from California for the brown drake hatch. My brother was not with me. My brother does not like fishing spring creeks. I was with Elaine. She paints landscapes while I fish. Silver Creek is the best spring creek.

One day the fishing was slow. The lawyer sat in the canvas chair drinking a beer. I put my rod against the fence.

His name was Greg. He fished the brown drake hatch.

"I've seen your rig," I said.

"I had a different rig before that," he said. "I've been coming eight years."

"I've made it the last few myself," I said.

"Like a beer?"

He was a divorced lawyer from Portland. He wasn't lawyering anymore, he said. He was on permanent disability. He could not stand for more than thirty minutes. His legs hurt so much. His spine hurt so much. It was a childhood affliction. It was getting worse, he said. He had had operations. He had almost died.

Silver Creek was perfect, smooth for miles, slick and clear and clean. You could skip a stone across it underhand.

He fished in a tube harness. I saw him in the tube, floating, casting down and across, a hunched, sun-baked yellow piece of flotsam beneath the blue Idaho sky.

"I have time," he said. He laughed. "So I'm a trout bum. I sold the house. I sold the car. I sold it all. When the hatch is done here, I'm driving to the Henry's Fork. The hatch will be there too. Give me your e-mail address. I'm writing my fishing chronicles. It feels good to write. My friends want me to write."

A bed was at the rear of the trailer, together with a chemical toilet, a shower, a small sofa and table, a tiny stove and refrigerator. The nose of the trailer was customized for fly tying. He had had two windows cut in, one on either side, and when he sat tying, he could see the stream. He could see birds and animals. At night he could see moonlight on the water, a trout rise and the ring of the rise disappear into the shadows along the bank. Young guys sleep in cars or a pup tent. They sleep on the ground. Greg was getting old. He had afflictions. He set himself up, in a lawyerly way. It was organized. He couldn't stand in a courtroom. He couldn't stand in the creek. He took a half dozen Vicodin to stop the pain. But he could float. I watched him from the road, floating alone, his graphite rod a bright sting against the blue Idaho sky.

One evening he baked Cornish game hens for us. The hens were stuffed with wild rice. We had red wine. We had asparagus. We had white sweet corn and sourdough French bread from a market in Bellevue, where Elaine and I stayed. For dessert we had chocolate lava cake. We sat at the table in the trailer. A stereo was built into a cabinet. He played Eric Satie and Claude Debussey. He played Poulenc. Outside, the creek moved silently. In the half-light it was silver gray. The moon was a platter upon the surface. The tying vice at the mahogany counter in the nose of the trailer was silver too. It was a quiet silver. He was a trout bum from Portland. He had no wife. He had no house or job. It was a trout bum's life, in a glorious, lawyerly way. We traded flies. I gave him my e-mail address.

I liked listening to him. He talked about himself or about trout. The vocabulary of his failed marriage, his illness and travels rolled from him as easily as the blue smoke of the cigars he lit, one after the other. He never lost a case in court, he said. He said he loved his kids and forgave his wife. He talked about how many pills he took to stop the pain. There was time, he said. It was time enough.

He talked about leasing the red cabin a half-mile up the creek from the access. He had a dream about friends coming to fish that part of the creek. No one fished it. It was on private land. He talked about what he got from disability and how he spent the money. He hid nothing. We were invited for dinner the following year. He was a lawyer from Portland. There are different lawyers. Greg had no precedent.

One day I went early to the access to have a cup of heavy, dark coffee according to Greg. The trailer was gone.

At the end of the month, the first issue of the Chronicles appeared in my e-mail box. A quote from William Blake was at the top of the first page: "The road of excess leads to the palace of wisdom."

A litany of notable birds and mammals he had seen followed: Bullock's Oriole, Cinnamon Teal, Common Merganser, Golden Eagle, Western Tanager, Coyote, Muskrat, Antelope, Otter, Elk. The list went on. The recipe for June was included. It was stuffed Cornish game hens. He wrote how to prepare them. Each day of the month was there, where fished, what used, how fished, how many caught, how many lost. If he met anyone or talked to anyone, he wrote what was talked about. At the end of the day he wrote what he ate, what CD he listened to. He wrote about what he read before sleep. He read stories about fishing. On June 10th he had a discussion at the Henry's Fork. Another fisherman said that a real fly fisherman only casts a dry fly to rising fish. Greg smiled. He told the fisherman he enjoyed drifting soft hackles beneath the surface into a pod of rising trout. He said he had been known to thread (I could see him smiling through the words) a bare hook through the abdomen of a grasshopper and to float the grasshopper down, legs kicking, into the shadows beneath tall trees. There was one page for each day, thirty pages in all. On the page for June 8th Elaine, Greg and I sat down in the trailer to baked Cornish game hens stuffed with wild rice. Outside, the moon shone upon the creek.

"A nice couple," the Chronicles said. "They're divorced too." That night Greg read again the one about the young man who fished alone in the woods. He read it twice. "Then I had a Manhattan," the Chronicles said, "Then I had another Manhattan. It was one too many. I couldn't sleep."

In Montana at the end of July I told my brother about the disabled lawyer from Portland who was now a trout bum. I told him that when we returned home in August, I would find in my e-mail box thirty-one days of size 18 mayflies drifting, drag free, into the jaws of enormous trout. I would find Beethoven, Copeland and cabernet. I would find sparrows, hawks, eagles, white-tailed deer, beaver and squirrels. I would find the wind and the sun and braised duck steaming upon the table. I would see moonlight upon the water. Before sleep, the Old Man might fish the sea again or the trout stream of his youth, alone, without father or brother. Cramped by pain, Greg floated in that yellow tube. The water was to his waist. He couldn't see the fly. Ahead, in the darkness, something Cretaceous rose.

My brother yawned.

"Let's get something to eat," he said. "I'm starved."

The Chronicles for July did not come. Through the long, black days of winter, I tied flies and waited for the sun. On Memorial Day we were at Silver Creek for the brown drake hatch. The trailer was not there.

I took the dirt road along the creek to the general store at Picabo, where the creek meets State Highway 20. Bob Monaghan, who runs the store, stood behind the counter. Last season Bob took six-dozen of Greg's flies to sell at the store. He wanted six dozen more.

"Where is he?" I asked.

"He's not coming," Bob said.

"What do you mean? What happened?"

"They found him in the tube," Bob said, "Up in Canada somewhere, floating along. He was full of drugs."

I looked at him.

"I don't know anything about anything," Bob said.

Photographs of Hemingway were on the back wall. He lived here at the end. I went to the wall. In one of the photographs Gary Cooper was with Hemingway. Bud Purdy was between them holding a pair of field glasses. Bud owned the ranch on Silver Creek where I sometimes fished. Cooper and Hemingway held shotguns.

Before we left, I went to the cemetery outside Ketchum where Hemingway is buried. I looked at the granite slab.

It's time to go on around.

My Old Man

I was a young man when Hemingway blew his head away with a shotgun. So, naturally, I figured, I'll hit 61, and it's over. Later, my father fell down from a heart attack in the house of a woman who was not my mother. That was the closer. He was 61. I had two fathers, a literary father and a biologic father. I never knew either one of them.

Yet, like an arrow to a target, life found meaning. Do what you must to eat. Go forward. Do the work. Work is everything. Don't look back. If you look back, the two of them will be there, in the dark and dirty place, drinking beer together.

I hit 61. Then I hit 71. In a few months I'll be 73 years old. I've looked back. No one is there. The café is boarded up. It's out of business.

What do you do when fate collapses, when the sense of a final paragraph, a last chapter vanishes into the indefiniteness of each morning's empty page?

You look, and you ask, what have I done? It's natural for an old man to ask, what have I done?

I went to school, and I wrote. I got married, and I wrote. I had a family, I taught, and I wrote. I got a divorce and wrote. I met many women, and through each I wrote, and then I found the one, so that I wished I had not had the others. She's old now too.

And I wrote.

I do not remember ideas, concepts, plans or purposes. I remember people. I remember places. I remember what I did, where I sat. I remember friends who, for some reason, were no longer friends, and then died. I remember where we were and what we had to eat and what we talked about while we were eating. It's hard to think that the café is closed, that it is dusty and dark and nobody goes there anymore.

A ghost, I wander. I find photographs whose edges are black. And where it begins, every time, is that I am in the second grade, it is summer, and I am out in the back yard casting the scarred bamboo fly rod my father found in a garage sale. The rod has no reel, so there is no line, but I arc the rod, forward and back. The bamboo, which is a coppery brown, still glints in the light. In my imagination the line turns away, unrolling beautifully in a narrow loop. The leader brings the fly over. The fly lands like a wisp by the rock made wet by steel-gray water that is only the chipped stone of my driveway. The gold, orange and yellow trout rises to the fly, and I am off, yielding line, stumbling down the river, to land, finally, in a quiet backwater under a cottonwood tree, which is only my old man's faded green Hudson, the biggest trout any boy has ever caught. It was there, in the deep promise of consciousness, that I decided to write.

We went, my old man and I, into the Sierra to fish for trout. We camped by the rivers. We hiked the streams. I learned about where trout hid, what trout ate, how to present artificial bugs, one tied above the other, to betray a trout's instinct for life. My old man always caught more trout than I, and then, after a time, because he smoked too much, drank too much and got too fat, he sat in a flat-bottomed aluminum boat on the tiny lakes near our streams, and I rose with the dawn, stalking and stumbling until the afternoon sun drove me back to camp, where, invariably, I found my old man snoring inside the tent, his shoes off, empty bottles of beer stacked against the ice chest, a pile of Chesterfields crushed into the lid of a coffee can.

Then one day my old man said, "I can't do it anymore."

"What do you mean?" I asked.

"Too old," he declared. He was in his early fifties. I was just out of Berkeley. "Take the gear," he said. "You're on your own."

There were a few guys I thought might be interested in fly-fishing. I let them use the old man's stuff. We went up and tried it, but no one stayed. It was work. There were mosquitoes. The ground was hard. The pancakes were crusted with fat from the bacon. So after a while I joined a club. They had one in town, even then. Everyone believed he was a pro, with expensive equipment and clothes bought from a New York catalog. There were always too many guys. The club fished this stream. The club fished that stream. They got in the way. They ruined the holes. I told the old man.

"It's too bad," he said. "I wish I could."

But his eyes were far away. He was drinking more and smoking two packs a day and fatter than ever. So I figured, if I want to be a fly fisherman and I want to do it right, that is, with any sense of truth and beauty, I'll have to fish alone.

I thought, what happens if you slip, crack your head against a rock and float face down above the trout? Who would save your ass? Or you put your foot over a log, hiking past the rapids, and there's a rattlesnake, which proceeds to introduce its fangs to your leg through the soft rubber of your boot. What then? Or food poisoning. Or suppose the car won't start or there's a bear or a mountain lion or you break an arm, your right arm. I was tentative. I looked over my shoulder. I missed a lot of strikes.

Yet I fished my way up through the wife and the children, through the students, until my father went down on that living room floor, and then the divorce, then the others, until that one, and I learned that all fishing is alone.

I fished in Alaska and Chile. I fished in Canada and New Zealand. I fished the chalk streams of England, the spring creeks of Montana, Idaho, Oregon and Wyoming. I went back East and fished where fly-fishing began in America. I fished Hat Creek in Northern California. I tied my own flies. I wrote.

Hemingway was a fly fisherman too. The only thing of his I read anymore is the one about the boy, the trout and the burned-over country.

The baggage is pitched from the baggage car of the train. He picks it up—it's all he needs—swings it against his back and adjusts the straps.

The town is burned, the foundation stones opened by the fire. The hills are burned too. The grasshoppers are black from living on the burned-over land. Everything he remembers has gone down under the fire, but it can't all be gone. He knows that. Fire burns everything, but it can't burn everything at once. Up the road beyond the blackened hills are the sweet grass and fern. If he goes far enough, he can make his camp beneath green pines and white stars, a good camp, where brown trout, big headed, gold and yellow, hold steady in the deep current of the stream with wavering fins. Beyond the burned-over country, he will make his camp, alone, in the good place, where nothing can touch him.

It is unnecessary now to catch trout. I have stood mornings and evenings, my fly rod in the crook of my arm, watching the flow of bright water. Often a rainbow or a brown trout has fallen for the ruse, and I have flipped the fly away. I laugh at myself. It seems silly and unnatural, yet grand, for there will come a time when I will stand only in imagination, as I did when I was a boy, and they will come behind closed eyes. It does not matter, finally, if the hook has no point.

At the end of his story Hemingway puts off fishing the swamp. He sits on a log and smokes a cigarette after a day's success on the stream. The stream narrows ahead. It goes under a big cedar. Beyond are more cedars, their branches stacked together, close to the ground so that walking is impossible. There is only one way to fish the swamp. He has to get down into the water. He has to wade up to his shoulders. He has to catch big trout where it is impossible to land them, where there is no light.

Hemingway did fish it. In his life he fished it. But he got trapped, far back inside, where the branches touch the water, and the bottom is soft. The black things came, like crocodiles, and ate him alive. My old man did not know of the swamp. He had the catastrophe of life.

I stood in a high Montana stream two years ago, when I turned 71, and there it was, what had held me together, day by day, as all the days roll into the abyss. I looked at what I had done and at what was left.

To remain seems rather futile, wouldn't you say, to have one more meal, to know one more taste, when eating never makes you full; to write one more paragraph, no matter how lovely the illusion, and always return. Would we sit at a table if the food had no flavor? Would we move a hand across a blank page if what we left there were ordinary? Was there no way out from under Hemingway and my old man?

Upstream the water came beneath a wooden bridge, the river widening and widening, bright and brighter, with a whitewater heat that danced in the light; and, before me, a bubbling torrent, a fury of sound, like the sound of iron wheels dampened in a tunnel, a tumble of blue water, a sep- arate sun, and an unhurried, greater distance, where a gray eagle turned, head lowered in thoughtless desire, hunting for prey.

I looked about. I'm fishing alone. I'm fishing Harold Bro-mely's ranch, and Harold isn't here. But I'm here, and every-thing that I am is here, and everything that I am not.

I am in the dark place, looking for reasons. The current wells up beneath my arms. The black things come with open jaws.

The removal from life of the blueprint of tragedy and folly by which everything is measured, therein lies the secret of the eagle's eye. That is what drains the swamp and nails shut the door of memory. Hemingway missed it. My old man missed it.

I'm in the river, a fly rod in one hand, a pencil in the other. It's enough.

About the Author

Richard Dokey's stories have won awards and prizes, have been cited in Best American Short Stories, Best of the West, have been nominated for the Pushcart Prize and have been reprinted in numerous regional and national literary reviews and anthologies. Pale Morning Dun, his collection of short stories, published by University of Missouri Press, was nominated for the American Book Award. His writings have appeared most recently in Adelaide Literary Magazine, Alaska Quarterly Review, Grain(Canada), Natural Bridge, Southern Humanities Review, Lumina and The Chattahooc-hee Review.

Acknowledgments:

Fly Fishing the River Styx, Fish Story, SOUTH DAKOTA REVIEW;
Big Two-Hearted River: Part III, Something Happened, Motel Man,
WEBER-THE CONTEMPORARY WEST; Patagonia, CONNECTICUT REVIEW;
Oedipus in Montana, CHARITON REVIEW; The One That Got Away, HINDSIGHT;
Fisherman, PRAIRIE WINDS; O, Brother!, THIRD COAST; Pale Morning Dun,
MISSOURI REVIEW; My Old Man, PHANTASMAGORIA; Match the Hatch, BROAD
RIVER REVIEW; Chasing the Whale, RUBBERTOP REVIEW

Made in the USA
Middletown, DE
23 April 2019